UNSP⚡RKED

3

PANIC!

CORINNA TURNER

PRAISE FOR CORINNA TURNER'S BOOKS

LIBERATION: nominated for the *Carnegie Medal Award 2016.*
ELFLING: 1st prize, Teen Fiction, *CPA Book Awards 2019*
I AM MARGARET & *BANE'S EYES:* finalists, *CALA Award 2016/2018.*
LIBERATION & *THE SIEGE OF REGINALD HILL:* 3rd place, *CPA Book Awards 2016/2019.*

Corinna Turner was awarded the **St. Katherine Drexel Award** in **2022.**

PRAISE FOR *ELFLING*

I was instantly drawn in
EOIN COLFER, author of *Artemis Fowl*

PRAISE FOR *DRIVE!*

What a terrifying futuristic world Turner has created!
I am a huge fan of this author and am always impressed
with how different all her stories are. Look forward to
the next one in this series!
LESLEA WAHL, author of award-winning *The Perfect Blindside*

A cross between Jurassic World *and* Mad Max!
Fun, fast paced. And sets up an incredible new world.
I read it three times in two days!
STEVEN R. MCEVOY, BookReviewsAndMore Blogger
and Amazon Top 500 Reviewer

Wow! So suspenseful you won't be able to put it down!
KATY HUTH JONES, author of *Treachery and Truth*

A fun read! Great tension ...
Jurassic Park *fans will love this short!*
CAROLYN ASTFALK, author of *Rightfully Ours*

Very short, but extremely exciting. ... The action is brutal, but it
drags you in and doesn't let you go until you hit the last page.
ASHLEY STANGL

ALSO BY CORINNA TURNER:

I AM MARGARET series
For older teens and up

Brothers *(A Prequel Novella)**
1: I Am Margaret*
1: Io Sono Margaret (Italian)
2: The Three Most Wanted*
3: Liberation*
4: Bane's Eyes*
5: Margo's Diary*
6: The Siege of Reginald Hill*
7: A Saint in the Family
'The Underappreciated Virtues of Rusty Old Bicycles' *(Prequel short story) Also found in the anthology:* Secrets: Visible & Invisible*

I Am Margaret: The Play *(Adapted by Fiorella de Maria)*

UNSPARKED series
For tweens and up

Main Series:
1: Please Don't Feed the Dinosaurs
2: A Truly Raptor-ous Welcome
3: PANIC!*
4: Farmgirls Die in Cages*
5: Wild Life
6: A Right Rex Rodeo
7: FEAR[†]

Prequels:
BREACH!*
A Mom With Blue Feathers[†]
A Very Jurassic Christmas
'Liam and the Hunters of Lee'Vi'

FRIENDS IN HIGH PLACES series
For tweens and up

1: The Boy Who Knew (Carlo Acutis)*
2: Old Men Don't Walk to Egypt (Saint Joseph)*
3: Child, Unwanted (Margaret of Castello)

Do Carpenter's Dream of Wooden Sheep? *(Spin-off, comes between 1 & 2)*

1: El Chico Que Lo Sabia (Spanish)
1: Il Ragazzo Che Sapeva (Italian)

YESTERDAY & TOMORROW series
For adults and mature teens only
Someday: A Novella*
Eines Tages (German)
1: Tomorrow's Dead[†]

OTHER WORKS

For teens and up
Elfling*
'The Most Expensive Alley Cat in London' (Elfling *prequel short story*)

For tweens and up
Mandy Lamb & The Full Moon*
The Wolf, The Lamb, and The Air Balloon (Mandy Lamb *novella*)

For adults and new adults
Three Last Things *or* The Hounding of Carl Jarrold, Soulless Assassin*
A Changing of the Guard
The Raven & The Yew[†]

[†] **Coming Soon**
* **Awarded the Catholic Writers Guild** *Seal of Approval*

PANIC!

CORINNA TURNER

DARRYL

An absurd sense of betrayal grips me as I stand, with Kiko—subdued and silent—clinging to my shoulder, staring and staring at the electric fence. *Our* fence. Dad's pride and joy, the twin Renfield Ozone 4 he spent such a chunk of his savings on when Harry and I were little, to keep us all safe.

How can it have failed us like this?

No sign of a breach marred the fence's readings when we got up, no alarms triggered, no malfunctions logged, *nothing*. I'm surely trapped in a nightmare because it's all so *impossible*. How were no alarms set off? And how could a Dakotaraptor, even a small one, get through that tiny hole? We're talking about something larger than a big cow, albeit skinnier and more flexible. It doesn't make sense.

"Darryl?" Maurice Carr, our neighbor, rests a hand on my shoulder, his voice strained. Over by the four trucks, Deb, the oldest Swayle girl, is hugging my thirteen-year-old brother Harry, her sisters clustered around them. Our other neighbors, Riley Wahlburg and his fourteen-year-old son, Fred, gather disconsolately around Dad's bloodied and scratched truck as though if they keep examining the damage long enough it might mean something else. Fred keeps glancing across at Harry, like he wants to comfort him but doesn't know how.

Sandra Wahlburg's already headed to the farmhouse with Tina Swayle to break the news to our new stepmom, Carol. I should head over there too. I should.

"It's not possible." I hear my words without consciously making the decision to speak them.

"Eh, I dunno." Uncle Mau tilts his grey Stetson back to scratch his slightly receding brown hair. "No mystery why the alarms didn't go off, I reckon."

"No?"

"'Course not. This fence is only alarmed every five strands. The hole, by the worst luck, simply didn't touch any of the alarm wires."

He's right, of course. On the very latest fences, like his, every single strand is alarmed. "But surely it would've affected one of the readings!"

He shrugs. "I'd've said so too, but I guess not."

"It couldn't *fit*. What made those marks. *It couldn't*."

"Guess it did, sweetie. Have you never had a bullock or frisky young 'saur squeeze through some hole you couldn't believe possible? I sure have. Guess this is why the new fences don't leave anything to chance."

I still just can't… "Okay, so it got in. But how did it get" —my throat closes—"how did it get Dad *out?*" 'Cause he's not in here. We've looked and looked.

"Oh, sweetie." Uncle Mau's voice goes very low and vibrates slightly. "Don't…don't think about that,

Darryl. Don't."

In other words, the thing just pulled and pulled and…without setting off the alarms? All my confidence in our fence has evaporated, every certainty flown away. How could the dang thing fail us like this? Now Dad's gone.

Eaten, whispers a chill voice in my head.

Gone is bad enough.

"If he saw the hole" — my voice wobbles; I'm a hair from breaking down — "why'd he leave his rifle in the truck?"

"Guess he thought what we thought, sweetie. That nothing big enough to be dangerous could've got through it. Probably thought nothing *had* got through. He took a good look around and then just got out to fix it. Same way I'd've done."

My throat feels so tight. Tears prick my eyes, but I don't want to cry. I mean, sure, no question, I'm going to cry some time. In my room. Or maybe when it's just Harry. But I don't want to cry *now.* I've got to be strong. Carol knows nothing about farm life. In a way, as far as the farm's concerned, I'm in charge now. I've *got* to be strong.

Swallowing hard, I turn away from the fence and march over to Dad's farm truck. I grab the fence key fob from where it lies on the dash, put Kiko, with his four long, trailing wing-limbs — and tail — safely inside and shut the door, then lift a roll of wire and the fence toolkit from the back. Thing must've gotten Dad before he'd even unloaded what he needed. Moment he opened the door, I guess. That's where all the blood and claw marks are.

Mau and Riley gather around as I turn towards the fence again.

"What are you doing, hon?" asks Riley.

"I'm fixing the fence; what do you think?"

"You don't have to do that, sweetie." Uncle Mau waves awkwardly towards the farmhouse. "We'll do that. You should take Harry in and get some tea, the both of you."

I want to scream at him, at them both, at the universe. I grit my teeth and try to speak evenly. "I'm *fixing* our fence, okay?"

We've already taken photos of everything on our ScreamerBands, so there's no reason to wait any longer. I march over to the hole, dump the things and head to the nearest upright post to power down the damaged section. Just the inner. I'll have to go between-fence to mend the outer hole. Mau and Riley can cover me, if they're so keen to help. They're hovering anxiously a few feet behind me and it's annoying.

It's not a difficult repair. The hole's so small there's no point replacing the entire length, so I splice new wire on to patch the gap, securing it thoroughly with the heat crimps. When I power the section back up, the readings are normal—but then, they were before.

I power it down again and unclip the access clips from the post, sliding out through the slit.

"We can—" Uncle Mau begins, but I ignore him. He sighs. "Alright, we've got your back."

I know I should give him a break. Both of them. They've just lost their oldest, bestest friend. But I've just lost my dad, and I don't know what to do. Except mend our traitorous fence.

So that's what I do.

HARRY

When Darryl's satisfied with the fence repair, she finally retrieves Kiko and lets Uncle Mau drive us back to the farmhouse in his shiny ride. Riley follows with Dad's truck, while Fred brings their vehicle along with Mau's sons Bentley and Royce, who showed no signs of wanting to come with Darryl and me. Guess they don't know what to say.

Darryl and I get out, and we both stand in front of the front door, looking at the house…where Dad isn't waiting.

This can't be happening…

Yes, it can. When I was four, that stupid accident took Mom from us. Bentley and Royce's mom, Sarah, got sick and died a few years ago. Just weeks ago, we watched as that longneck smashed down on that family's car, killing every last one of them. We thanked God it wasn't us and went on with life, 'cause, well, that's life, isn't it? And today it's us again. It's Dad.

Darryl turns towards me and hugs me, hard. I hold her back, until I'm afraid I'm going to cry again. I don't want to, not with everyone still here, watching. Darryl hasn't cried and I want to be as strong as she is.

"Okay, let's…" Her voice shakes. "Let's go and see Carol."

Oh heck, Carol… She's only lived out-city a matter of weeks. How will she cope with this? She and Dad were, like, super-gooey in love. Now she's stuck outSPARK on a farm without him, with two kids who aren't hers but kinda are, now.

I can't reply. My tongue's locked itself. Somehow I manage to follow Darryl as she steps inside and walks to the family room.

The steel shutters are half-closed against the morning sun, leaving the room striped with brightness and shadow. Carol's sitting on the sofa with Sandra and Mrs. Swayle on either side of her. Carol's eyes are red and blotchy, her face so pale it contrasts starkly with the arm Sandra has around her shoulders. Tears trickle slowly down her cheeks, a glazed look in her eyes.

"We've never known such a thing," Mrs. Swayle is

saying gently. "It's quite unprecedented. Not that that's any comfort, of course. Here, have another sip." She tries to coax Carol into drinking some more...sweet tea?

"No!" Fretfully, Carol bats at the mug, spilling tea on the floor. "How can...how can you all be so calm about this! Why don't you *do* something? You haven't even *found* him yet!"

Darryl's shoulders lift as she draws a deep, deep breath. She passes Kiko to me, ignoring his squawk of protest, then steps forward. Mrs. Swayle slides over into the armchair, letting Darryl settle beside Carol and slip her arm around her in an awkward half-hug.

"Carol, we want to do something, we really do, but...there's...there's just nothing more that can be done. He's..." Her voice wobbles. "He's *gone*, Carol. And we're not calm, we're distraught but...nothing can change facts. We have to..." Her voice drops very low and quivery. "We have to go on with things. Only thing we can do. Go on."

Go on. Yeah, that's how life works. Especially out here. Pretty soon someone's going to have to go around the 'saur stock and check on last season's calves and milk the cow and the hens will need feeding and...and it'll all just go on. Without Dad.

A huge lump blocks my throat and a triceratops is stomping on my chest. I raise a hand quickly to stroke Darryl's nervous pet, trying to distract myself. The little quadravian can sense the tension, no question.

It'll all go on without Dad. But…that is what Dad would want. I know *that*. Things *must* go on. If they don't…what's the point to *anything?* Even in the city, things go on, right? I guess they just wring their hands more beforehand.

"Go on?" Carol gasps it, incredulity on her face. "*Go on*? How can you just sit there and…" She breaks down into great shuddering sobs, throwing herself into Sandra's arms.

"Oh, shhhh. Oh, hon, shhh. Don't mind Darryl and us'uns. It's just our country way, y'know, to be all matter-o'fact about things. Don't mind us. We're just heartbroken, too, y'know."

Darryl shoots me a miserable look. I stare back numbly. I don't know what to say to Carol either. I don't know what to say to anyone. Dad's gone. It's just us now. Darryl and me. And Carol. *We* understand how we feel, and we don't need to sit around and talk about it. But it feels like Carol's on the other side of a canyon, and we don't know how to build a bridge.

Uncle Mau and Riley round up Fred, Bentley, and Royce and start giving them instructions in an under-tone about going out and checking what needs doing on the farm and getting on and doing it. I want to go and help them. I want it more than anything. To be doing something. But I shoot a look at Carol and stay put. I want to be busy 'cause of how much I *do* care, but I'm not sure she'll take it that way. Darryl shoots a look after them, like she feels the same way.

With a wary look at Carol, Mrs. Swayle—also in an undertone—sends her daughters into the kitchen to fix breakfast, and Uncle Mau and Riley head into Dad's little office to start preparing a Fatal Accident Notification. Darryl remains on the sofa next to Carol, occasionally patting her back cautiously, looking thoroughly trapped and helpless. I know how she feels.

Eventually, a ping issues from the three linked ScreamerBands in the room—Darryl's, Carol's, and mine. Someone with a pass code has just come through the gates. As the vehicle draws up in the yard, Darryl lifts her head and mouths, *"Father Ben."*

Then she leaps up and dashes out of the room.

DARRYL

I've got to stop him. That's all I'm thinking as I race through the front door. I've got to stop him stepping into the house with some booming, cheerful remark about the happy day ahead. The marriage blessing that will never happen now. I've just got to. I can't hear it, I can't. And Carol…she really mustn't have to hear it. She's so…so…upset's too simple, but yeah.

Sure enough, Father Ben's smiling as he gets out of

the driver's side of his van, his white teeth gleaming against his dark skin. But the smile drops away as his eyes fall on me.

"Darryl? Is everything—?"

He doesn't get any further, because I've thrown my arms around him, and I'm crying and clinging like I'm drowning. I didn't mean to, but I am. I guess he can be strong for a few minutes instead of me. He's been such a gentle, reliable presence in my life since I was little.

"Ah, Darryl, sweetheart, what's wrong?"

He rubs my back and shushes me, until finally I manage to gulp, "It's Dad."

"What's happened? Is he…sick?" His wary tone doesn't sound hopeful.

I shake my head—wait, he'll think I mean Dad's okay—I change it to a nod, sniffing as I try to force the words out.

"Dang raptor come in and ate him." Harry's voice, small and flat, comes from the front door, just before Kiko lands on the back of my head.

Father Benedict's breath goes out in a long hiss. "Ah, no. No, no, no…"

"Yes," I sniff. "This morning, when he was checking the fence. There's blood and claw marks and a hole, and he's gone and…and…" I trail off. And life's just imploded in a way even Mom's death didn't cause.

"Oh, my word." He hugs me tightly for a moment,

then frees an arm to draw Harry in for a quick hug too. Kiko stays on top of my head, out of the way. "Oh my. God rest his soul. You poor things. But you have such a good fence…"

"Total freak accident." Uncle Mau leans against the doorframe now, a thumb hooked through his belt, his face drawn and tired. "One of those things you wouldn't think possible until it happens and then you can justabout see how it is."

"But…is it safe?"

Uncle Mau shrugs. "Yeah. I mean, I don't see what one could change. Chances of it happening once were so slim, *twice* just isn't worth worrying about. Only thing would be to put in a brand new fence, and…well."

Cost. Prohibitive.

"Overreaction, anyway." Riley looks around Mau's shoulder. "I don't reckon it's going to happen again. Unlucky enough it happened once, if you ask me."

"I'll say," mutters Mau sourly, glaring at Father Ben.

"You can't blame me unless there's a God; don't try to have it both ways, Maurice." Father Ben's usually more patient with Uncle Mau's atheism, but I guess he's upset too. He looks at me again. "How's poor Carol?"

"Upset. Uh…obviously, I guess. We…we can't seem to…say the right thing." I can't help eyeing him hopefully. I mean, he's been a rural priest since I was about five, but he was a city-man, born and bred, before that.

He hugs me again, one-armed, because his other arm's still around Harry. "Aw, Darryl, sweetie, I'm not sure it's really possible to say 'the right thing' at a time like this."

"Yeah," mutters Harry, "but everything we say is, like, really *wrong*."

Father Ben sighs and gives him another squeeze too. "Yeah. It's hard. Well, shall we go in and see how she is?"

I'd rather go and check on some stock. I'd really, really *like* to go and check on some stock, in fact. But one of the boys or the Swayles is bound to have done it by now. I guess the least I can do for Carol is make an effort by sticking around, even if I can't say the right thing to her.

HARRY

"Now, don't you worry about a thing," Riley tells Carol as, shortly after midday, the Wahlburgs head back to their own farm. "We'll be along tomorrow morning to help with everything and see how you are."

Half an hour later, we're back at the front door again, seeing Uncle Mau off. "Don't you worry," he says to Carol. "We'll all be over to help out each day just so long as you need it. Many hands make light work. You just concentrate on looking after yourself, now."

Mrs. Swayle already took her daughters home. Her best iguanodon mare had started to lay earlier and she needs to check on her. But she said they'd be along tomorrow, too.

"Looking after myself?" sniffs Carol, watching their truck drive away.

"He's right, you know." Father Ben rests a gentle hand on her shoulder and steers her back inside. "Why don't you lie down and try to rest awhile?"

"Lie down?" Carol's tearful voice floats back out the door to us. "When…when William…when William's…"

I glance at Darryl. "Had we, er, better go and check on things?"

She shoots a guilty look at the house, stroking Kiko's head soothingly, but nods. "Yeah, let's go check everything."

We hurry away towards the nearest 'saur barn, towering above us, its walls clad in smooth no-climb metal. Dad carefully maintained the steel shutters and sturdy door on every barn, ensuring each can be locked-down almost as securely as the farmhouse if there's a breach. Much good that did him.

The thought of Dad brings a hard spiky lump to my chest, like I've swallowed an armadillion's tail club, so I talk to try and take my mind off it. "I'm glad they're all coming back tomorrow. No way you and I can get it all done."

"Yeah, we've got good neighbors." Darryl's voice is soft and tense. "We'll have all the help we need until we can hire someone."

"Hire someone?"

"We'll have to. No way can you and I do everything D…everything that needs doing *and* keep up with our TuteApps even halfway."

Horrible to think of some stranger coming to live here instead of Dad.

"They can live in the loft apartment, though, right? Over the mammal barn?"

"Yeah, 'course."

Guess that's not quite so bad. Yeah? Who am I kidding? This just sucks, all of it. I can't believe Dad's…gone.

We go in through the door onto the obsoDeck and look down into the pens. A sickly edmontosaur and a lame iguanodon are the only critters in here at the moment. The edmo wanders up to the pen wall and raises its flat head hopefully.

Darryl leans over to scratch behind the big jaw. "Hello, girl. Are you feeling better?" Her voice quivers. Guess she's crying.

I move along a bit further to look down into the

second pen and after a while, Darryl joins me, her eyes
a little red.

"Is that a fresh dressing on her leg?" Her voice
sounds congested.

I peer through the gloom, "Yeah, I think it is."

She blows out a relieved breath. "Good. She's so
skittish I wasn't looking forward to just the two of us
changing it. I still think we should get rid—" She breaks
off suddenly.

Yeah, it's…it was…Dad who always wanted to
keep this iggy. She is an exceptionally fine mare, but
I've always figured Darryl's right—it's just not worth
the risk having a jumpy madam like her around. But I
don't like to say so right now, when Dad's…so I say
nothing.

We spend quite a while wandering aimlessly
around the farm, but everything's been done and done
well enough so, eventually, hearts sinking even further,
we head back to the house.

DARRYL

Father Ben meets us at the front door, placing a finger to
his lips. "I persuaded Carol to take a nap at last—with
the aid of a sleeping pill—and I think she's finally
dozed off. Let's try not to wake her. How about a cup of
joe?"

We settle in the family room with mugs of coffee and for a while a glum silence reigns. Father Ben stares into the depths of his cup and Harry stares at his boots, while Kiko clings to my shoulder, unusually quiet and still.

"Kids," says Father Ben at last, "I can stay about another hour, then I have to go."

My heart slides from the bottom of my belly right down into my feet, a dizzy panic gripping me. He has to leave so soon? The thought of Harry and me alone here with Carol, not knowing what to say…

He sees my expression and makes a face. "I'm really sorry. I wish I didn't, but I've got a wed…I have to say Mass east of Greenways tomorrow, and it's not something I can cancel. I can be back late tomorrow or the following day, though. Not sure which because there's a mechanic where I'm going so I'll get my van serviced. Then I can stay a day or so before I have to be down south. We can—" his voice softens even more— "we can plan a requiem, and I can come back again later next week for that; stay a little longer."

My heart sloshes around leadenly in my toes. Yeah, a requiem. We need to do that. "Do you think…" My voice comes out very small. "Do you think he's…okay?"

Father Ben reaches out and squeezes my shoulder. "Your father was a good man, and a faithful one, and to the best of my knowledge he was right with the good

Lord. Pray for him, of course, but don't worry yourself, all right? If he's not with your Mom already, I'm sure he will be soon enough."

I look down at my hands, feeling the hot tears flowing down my cheeks. Why did we have to lose Dad as well as Mom? Then I think of Janey and all my previous bottle-fed hatchlings. None of their mothers died; their moms just rejected one of their chicks and pushed them out of the nest and refused to feed them anymore. That's even worse, right? The world's a hard place. What is it Dad used to say?

"Adam shouldn't have eaten that dang apple."

Father Ben smiles sadly. "I won't argue with that."

HARRY

Darryl and I watch Father Ben's van until it's out of sight, only then returning to the house. Quietly. Carol's still asleep. The thought of facing her again makes me feel panicky. What will we say to her? Will she start crying again?

Father Ben never got a chance to tell her he'd have to leave, apparently, and it seemed pointless to wake her just to say goodbye. Let's hope that doesn't hurt her feelings.

"What do we..." I clear my throat. "What do we do now?"

Darryl glances at her ScreamerBand. "We might as well do the evening chores. It's slightly early but never mind. Then...then if Carol's not up I'll put something simple in the oven for supper. I know there's all the food Carol made for the...well, I guess she'd rather not see that, just yet. And...and then I'll go drive the fence." Her voice trails off in a squeak and she swallows hard.

Yeah. I guess that's her job now. Maybe I should offer to take over the bottle-feeding, when it's hatching time again. But I doubt she'll want that. She likes her little "orphans" too much. I can pick up other chores, I guess.

On our way outside, she pauses to check the readings on the house console more thoroughly than usual for this time of day, but all is okay. But my skin prickles as I walk around. I just don't feel safe quite the way I usually do.

By the time I've brought all the mammal-stock in, fed them and secured the barns for the night, then dropped the "no suck" barrier between the calf and our milk cow so we can have our share of the milk in the morning, Darryl's been around the 'saur pastures, checked last season's calves and driven the fence. Okay, to be honest, I'm twiddling my fingers slightly in the cowshed, waiting for her to get back so I don't have to go into the house on my own.

"Everything okay?" I ask her.

"It's all fine. Let's see if the food's done."

Darryl's just lifting a tray of 'saur nuggets and chips out of the oven when a noise comes from the doorway.

I spin around. Carol. I flip between, *phew, only Carol* and *eek, it's Carol; what shall I say?* I still feel kinda jumpy after what...after what happened this morning.

Darryl puts the tray down on a trivet and stares anxiously at Carol. "Hi, Carol. How are you feeling? Are you...okay?"

"Okay?" Carol's lip trembles.

"I mean...I know you're not *okay*, not like that," blurts Darryl. "I just meant...do you feel any better after a rest?"

"Better? He's still... William's still..." Carol swallows hard. She's clearly trying not to break down again, thank God.

"I know," says Darryl quickly. "I know. It's...it's just horrible." She stares around the kitchen desperately for a moment, swinging her arms, then looks at the steaming food. "D'you...d'you think you could manage a bite to eat? It's just something plain."

"I couldn't possibly eat a thing."

"But...you didn't have any lunch. Did you even have any breakfast?"

"William is—" Carol's voice rises sharply and breaks off. "How can you think about eating? Have you even noticed he's gone? Sitting down to breakfast like nothing had happened! And you had lunch, too? Don't you even..."

Darryl's throat works, her eyes glassy with unshed tears. "Of course we've noticed! Of course we care! But starving ourselves isn't going to bring him back! There's work to do; we have to eat!" She breaks off and swallows again, then speaks softly. "Please sit down with us and have something, Carol. Dad would want you to look after yourself, you know he would."

Carol says nothing, but after a long silence she takes some cutlery from the drawer and four plates from the plate rack, then turns towards the dining room.

"Oh, Father Ben had to go," Darryl says. "But he'll be back late tomorrow or first thing the next day."

Carol looks around, her eyes opening wide. "He's...he's *gone*?"

"Uh," Darryl looks taken aback by her expression. "Yeah. But he'll be back really soon."

"You mean there's no one *here*? Except us?"

"Um, no? Who would there be? We'll have to get a worker to help with things, of course, but I haven't even drafted an advertisement yet... Carol, what's wrong?"

Carol is shaking, her eyes wide. "Who...who's going to...to protect us from those...those *things*!"

"What *things*?" Darryl looks wary. "I drove the fence just now, everything's safe and secure. Uncle Mau and Riley figure if I check the fence with the drone each morning before doing the on-site inspection, that'll... that'll largely fix the...million-to-one problem, and I agree. We're perfectly safe."

"But Father Ben's gone!"

I frown and speak at last. "Carol, Darryl's far better protection from any nasty critter than Father Ben. I know he's got that raptor claw necklace hanging in the cab, but that was, like, a one-off, years and years ago. Darryl and I will look after you, no worries. Darryl's a crack shot. More important than being tall and broad shouldered, honestly."

"No!" The plates rattle together as Carol dumps them back on the worktop, shooting a glance out of the kitchen window at the sky. "No! We can't stay here alone! We can't! Come on! Grab your things! We've just enough time!"

"Time for what?" asks Darryl.

"Time to get home to Exception City before it's dark."

DARRYL

Harry's eyes widen. My head spins. "*What?* But *this* is home!"

"No." Carol shakes her head wildly, dropping the knives and forks on the work surface with a clatter that makes Kiko leap from my shoulder and swoop up to the curtain rod. "Obviously we can't stay. But I was going to wait a few days. Arrange things properly. But since Father Ben's gone... No, we must go tonight. I was going to let my brother stay in the apartment but he's not moved in yet, so we can go straight home."

A cold, tingly feeling sweeps over me. "*This* is home!" My voice comes out too loud, too harsh. "We can't *leave!*"

"We can't stay here on our own!"

"Why not?"

"It's too dangerous!"

"It's not! We're perfectly safe!" Now I sound shrill and frantic.

"Safe?" Carol's skin goes pale with...fear? Anger? "*Safe?* How can you look me in the face after what happened this morning and claim this place is *safe?*"

"It was a million-to-one—"

"Oh, just like the accident on the highway, I suppose!"

"It *was!*"

"No!" Carol raises both hands in a sharp sideways gesture, cutting me off. "It's not safe here. I thought since Father Ben seemed so capable we could straighten things out while we were on site, but no. He's gone, so let's each pack a bag and be ready in..." She glances at her ScreamerBand, then at the window. "In twenty minutes. We can get home before dark. Yes, we can. But we must hurry!"

"Carol"—desperation fills me—"you know it's a three-hour drive, unSPARKed, right? You're not used to driving unSPARKed. We should wait until tomorrow at least. Uncle Mau or Riley would come along; drive us, in fact." *And maybe,* I can't help thinking, *they might talk you out of it once you've survived one night here with just the three of us.*

Carol glances at the window again. Her face is chalk-white and her eyes dart nervously, like she's trapped between two horrors. "Better three hours and we're safe than stay here all night and still have that to come tomorrow," she says hoarsely and turns to the door.

"But who'll look after the farm?" Harry sounds bewildered.

"The neighbors are all offering to help. They'll see to things until...well, I guess you're right, Darryl. You'll have to hire someone."

"But if we're not here," protests Harry, "we'll need to hire at least two!"

"Oh, never mind about all that now! We can sort it out once we're home. Quickly, pack!" Carol heads through the door.

"But..." Harry's talking to thin air. He looks at me, his eyes wide. "Ryl? She's not...she's not serious!"

I swallow, my lips dry. "She is. She's too scared to

see reason." For a moment Dad's truck flashes through my mind, clawed and bloodied. "Hard to blame her, I guess," I mutter.

"But Ryl! We have to stay. Persuade her to let us stay!"

"She's not going to let us stay here on our own, Harry. Not right now." I ram my thumbs to my temples, trying to think.

"Look..." I speak slowly, the words like lead, "we've got to go with her now. But once Mau and Riley have found us someone trustworthy to be manager here, maybe she'll let us come back. We want to be on the farm—we need to be!—but she only came out here 'cause of Dad. It's crazy to make her stay, I guess."

"But...do you *want* to go live in the city?"

"Of course I don't! But...it'll just be temporary, okay?"

"Can't we get her to drop us at Uncle Mau's?"

It's tempting. It's so tempting. Pre-Carol, Maurice was always supposed to be our guardian if anything happened to Dad. But I picture Carol's white face—and Dad's if he knew we'd just let her drive off, on her own, today of all days, hurting and terrified. Alone.

"Carol's our family now." I try to speak firmly. "Let's get her home. Once she's back in...back in her natural environment and she feels better, then we can think about coming home, okay?"

24

"What if she won't let us come back?"

"We'll persuade her, okay? Come on, quickly, pack some things."

I whistle Kiko back to my shoulder, shepherd Harry up the stairs and into his room, then go into mine. I pull out a dusty carryall from underneath the bed, but then I just flop on top of it and sob, making Kiko climb up onto the bedpost and peer down at me anxiously.

Despite my bold words to Harry, despite knowing it's the only thing we can do, I've never dreaded the future more in my life. What if she *won't* let us come back? Okay, it's less than two years until I'm eighteen—more like one and a half—then I could come back without her say-so, but I couldn't leave Harry. *Five* years before he's eighteen! I can't even imagine living *one* year in-city.

No, she'll let us come back. She will.

Lord, please let her!

I sit up and wipe my face then stroke Kiko for a moment. He's been so stressed all day. When he calms down enough to climb onto my shoulder, I unzip the bag and hastily pile in clothes, toiletries, my claw necklace, my handPad with my TuteApp on it, and anything else useful my scattered attention falls upon. Then I gather Kiko's things quickly, his bowls and leash and packets of fruit and nuts, before putting him into his travel cage and fastening it securely.

"Darryl? Harry? Are you ready?"

I look around my room and swallow hard. "Coming."

Despite what I've grabbed, my room remains full of my things. My life. I want to stay so much. *Lord, please!*

Maybe she'll change her mind. Hoping desperately, I pick up the carryall in one hand and Kiko's cage in the other and carry them downstairs. Maybe when it actually comes to driving away, she'll decide she'd rather stay than risk it.

I put Kiko into the backseat of the road truck then load my carryall into the trunk. I return to the house and put my hand on the scanner for the gun locker.

Carol hurries back inside after putting her own bags in the truck and stares as I take out my rifle and slip on my ammo sash. "Should you be...be handling those without an adult to supervise you? I don't know enough about them..."

I look at her incredulously. "Carol, I had my first rifle when I was seven. We're about to go for a three-hour drive, unSPARKed. Who do you think's going to protect us if we have a problem?"

"Yeah," says Harry, coming down the stairs holding the bag he uses occasionally for sleepovers. "We could break down, you know? Or have an accident. Then raptors might show up, and we'd have to fend them off. Even a flat tire and we'd be stuck. Or we might meet a bull triceratops that'll spike us on its horns and flip us clean over. We wouldn't be driving away upside down, would we?"

Harry's definitely trying to scare her into staying, and she's gone so pale... But she just says weakly, "I suppose you'd better bring the firearms, then."

Looking disappointed, Harry trudges out to the truck then returns for his rifle. Carol follows him outside again, and I move to the HouseControl—then stop. I don't know exactly how long we'll be gone. So I can't just leave… I head to the family room and turn the key to the tabernacle closet, open the door and genuflect.

Father Ben's emphasized often enough that a home tabernacle is a privilege extended to rural families, but not a right, and that part of appreciating that is taking proper care of the Divine contents. I can't just drive off for…possibly *months*—please, Lord, no!—leaving the tabernacle occupied but abandoned.

I unlock the tabernacle door, genuflect again, then nervously pick up the golden pyx from inside. Dad takes it out any Sunday Father Ben's not here to say Mass, turning the knob to open the spiral lattice so we can have Adoration, but I've never touched it before.

In a drawer to the side I find the little bag-like veil Mom stitched years ago and slip it over the pyx, tying the drawstrings at the bottom to keep it on. The whole thing I put into a heavy waterproof case of waxed cotton, then I unzip the interior pocket of my jacket and slide it inside, re-fastening it securely. What's left of our little family may be retreating in confusion, but Our Lord will be with us.

Everything re-locked, I return to HouseControl, then pause for a moment. If only someone could persuade Carol to give it a chance for one night. Riley's not much of a persuader, but Mau…I should've sent him a message before packing. Too late now. But when I check the console, I see the flashing symbol that says a satellite is properly in range for once. I might actually be able to speak to him.

Swiftly, I tap through to the Carr farm profile and press the audio call button. It rings a few times, then:

"'Lo?"

"Bentley?"

"Yeah…oh, Darryl!" His voice goes tense and awkward.

"Yeah, it's me. Can I speak to your dad?"

"Nah, he went to see a man about something. D'you want him to call you back later if there's another signal-lock?"

"No, don't worry, we're —"

With a bleep, the call cuts off as the satellite passes out of effective audio range. Blast. Mau's out. So much for that faint hope.

I tap the controls to set the house to seal as soon as

the front door shuts and reluctantly head outside. Carol's already started the truck. Leaden-hearted, I close the door and watch the shutters snick into place. Then I move over to the truck and carefully perform the pre-travel checks, shaking the window grilles and checking the wheel-guards. How often Dad did this… my heart aches.

But Dad fixed everything back into place really securely after the "incident," so soon there's nothing to do but climb in. I wedge my rifle over the handbrake, where Dad's would usually go, and look at Carol.

"Hadn't I better drive, Carol?"

"You? You're too young. You don't have your license."

I shrug. "No, but I reckon I'm far more experienced than you driving unSPARKed, right? We can swap back before we reach the main highway. But the first section is all unmonitored minor roads. Bad surface and every-thing. No cops, no other traffic. Better if I drive, right?"

Carol wavers then shakes her head. "No, no, you've no license. I must drive."

I sigh then reach out to touch the statue of Saint Desmond the Hermit on the dashboard, acutely conscious of that precious lump tucked inside my jacket. Harry joins in as I recite the traveling prayer, but Carol's pulling away before we finish.

When we reach the fence, I touch the WhatHap box,

but all I can manage is: "Carol, Darryl, and Harold Franklyn traveling to Exception City." *To return…?* What can I say?

Carol drives across the outer pastures, veering to and fro along the track as she tries to put a few extra feet between us and any of our herbi'saurs grazing peacefully nearby.

"Carol, are you sure you wouldn't rather wait until tomorrow, get someone to drive us?"

"No!" She hunches over the wheel, staring tight-lipped at the road. "No, we'll get it all over with tonight. Tomorrow…tomorrow will be normal."

What, like everything with Dad and living out-city was just some sort of dream slash nightmare? I bite my tongue and start keeping a proper watch on our surroundings as we pass under the bottom strand of our outer fence.

Everything's quiet, though, the sky a clear, crisp early spring blue. We soon pass from the flat farmland, the brown winter grass just beginning to give way to bright spring green, into the expanse of craggy hill country that separates us from the main highway to Exception City. Carol drives slowly and cautiously around every bend, accelerating frantically down every straight, clearly worried about making it to Exception in the light. With reason. There's no doubt we're making much slower progress than usual. I keep my mouth shut, though. She won't let me drive and piling on the pressure isn't going to help.

"Iggies," reports Harry calmly, at last. "South-west."

"What?" Carol swerves violently.

"Hey, relax!" I clutch the door grip. "Just herbi'saurs like ours. A wild herd. They're a long way away."

Carol drives on, shooting glances up the valley we're crossing.

"See…" I try to speak soothingly. "Just like the ones at home. Nothing to worry about."

Despite my words she's sweating, her knuckles white around the wheel. *Oh Lord, help her to calm down!* This is crazy. Why wouldn't she wait one night and let Mau or Riley drive us?

HARRY

Kiko is rustling around in his cage so much Darryl finally glances over her shoulder at me. "Let him out, Harry. It's going to be several hours yet. He might as well have a bit more space."

Three more hours, at this rate, despite we've been going for most of an hour already. I do as she says and Kiko immediately climbs forward, half onto her shoulder and half on the seatback, and settles there. But after a while, he begins to sniff then climbs into the back again and noses at Carol's tote bag.

"What do you want in there, Kiko?" I ask him. "I don't think eyeliner would suit you."

Darryl's lip twitches as she turns to watch him. "He certainly smells something interesting."

"It'll be the food," says Carol, still hunched over the wheel.

Darryl's head jerks around. "The *what?*"

"The food you cooked. I threw it into some take-out bags so you could eat it en route. Seeing as how the two of you keep getting hungry."

Clearly flabbergasted, Darryl opens her mouth then closes it and purses her lips as though trying to decide how to respond. I guess Carol was trying to be nice. But seriously?

"It was kind of you to think of that, Carol," Darryl says at last, "but, uh, it's actually better not to travel with unsealed food in this sort of vehicle, you know. Especially meat. Let's get it eaten, shall we?"

"Better not? Why?" asks Carol, eyes darting from the road to Darryl. "*What* sort of vehicle?"

"A lightly-shielded one. You know, as opposed to something armored like a HabVi—uh, Habitat Vehicle, remember? And even they keep everything sealed or frozen or in a special fridge. It's just…better not to attract…undue attention. Not to worry. We'll have it eaten in a jiffy, won't we, Harry?"

"Sure will." My stomach's been rumbling since we left home, and Carol's driving so slowly that I'm more glad to find there's hot—well, once hot—food on board than anything, big no-no as it is.

Darryl, Kiko, and I dig in, though Darryl eats only half-heartedly. Although I thought I was hungry, now that I'm actually eating, I don't have as much appetite as I expected. Kiko gets the lion's share, though Darryl actually manages to feed the odd 'saur nugget to Carol, and soon we're food-free. The starch bags are bio-degradable, so Darryl lowers the window and pokes them through the grille and that's us de-fooded. A pack of raptors chasing us along the road a few miles for the heck of it because we smell good might not bother Darryl and I, but Carol…

Yeah. Not good. While we've got our heads together for a moment sorting the food, Darryl even whispers to me, "Stop reporting 'saur activity to me, unless it really matters, 'kay?"

Yeah, Carol really should've let Darryl drive. Better still, Uncle Mau.

Too late, now.

DARRYL
"Oh, where is that highway?" whispers Carol, after

we've driven another half hour, bumpetty-bump, twistetty-twist.

"Not far now." I try to sound cheerful. "It's just taking a bit longer because you're not familiar with the minor road. Once we get on the highway, we'll fly along."

Two hours on the highway, though. I shoot a glance at her. Sweat plasters wisps of hair to her face and she looks exhausted.

"There's a SPARKed rest area about ten minutes after we get on the highway. We can stop for a break."

Carol shakes her head. "No, or it will go dark before we get home."

"Does it matter, once we're on the highway? Highway control can see in the dark." I almost add that we've no chance of getting there before dark now anyway, but I bite my lip. I'll point that out when we're nearing the rest area. No point stressing her even more right now.

We round a rocky bend and there in the middle of the road…

"Carol, stop!"

Her eyes bulge and for a moment I'm afraid she hasn't taken in what I said. I grip her arm tightly and speak firmly. "Carol, just *pull to a halt*. It's a mare and they're not territorial. We just need to wait for her to wander off."

Breathing hard, shaking, Carol draws to a standstill.

I let out a relieved breath, peering at the triceratops ahead of us. Several feet taller than the truck, its huge frill and two long horns give it a fearsome appearance. But…

"Look, Carol. It's browsing on that fresh wild grass growing on the shoulder of the road. That's all it's interested in. Not us. It's barely even looked at us, has it?"

"*Darryl…*" Harry speaks in a low voice.

Yes, this is just a mare. But it's nesting season. How close are her herd's nesting grounds? They can't be right by the road or Highway Control would have sent some hunters to deal with the hazard, this being a fairly "major" minor road. So not close enough that she's likely to attack us. And I don't see any calves with her, so she's not one of the early hatchers. But the herd can't be far. And with nesting females you get…

I lick my lips. "Okay, Carol, she's turned sideways slightly. Let's just drive slowly past her, okay?"

"Wh-wh-what?"

"Just drive gently past her. She's not interested."

"C-can't we just w-wait for her to…g-go?"

"It's not necessary, really. Come on…"

"No, I-I'd rather wait."

Heck, I'm going to have to say it. "Carol, there's no other way around, and we don't want to linger here.

There'll be a bull somewhere not that far away."

"A *bull?* Male triceratops? They're…they're dangerous, right?'

Extremely. "They can be, uh, short-tempered. Best to avoid one if we can. So let's just ease on our way, okay?"

Hands shaking, Carol puts the truck in gear again, and we slide forward. I keep my hand on her arm, gripping it reassuringly. "Keep going, keep going, it's okay…"

The mare watches us pass then goes back to stuffing her face, no doubt keen to return to her nest as quickly as possible. With so many protective females all in one place—to say nothing of the protective bull—most herd herbi'saurs leave their nest periodically to graze.

We round the next corner and there's the area of flatter, open country that eventually ripples through a few more crags before coming out on the highway. "Nearly there, Carol," I tell her. After a few more twists and turns to descend, we've almost reached the valley floor when a shape moves out of the shadows at the base of the slope.

Another triceratops. We're definitely near a nesting site.

"It's the bull!" Carol's scream chokes off in her throat as though she's too scared to speak. Before I can respond, she spins the wheel and we're off the road, plunging down a slope to the left and thudding onto a flatter area with a creak of stressed metal.

I wince, terrified for our axles, even as I shout, "It's *not!* It's another female! *Carol!*"

She's not listening. The engine revs as she presses hard on the gas, clods of mud spinning past the windows as we gather speed.

I grab her arm again, shouting right in her ear. "Carol! Stop! It's just a mare! A *mare*. Harmless! Carol! Slow down! Slow down, okay?"

Her arm shakes under my hand but, gradually, her wide eyes relax a little and she shoots a look in my direction. "Darryl?"

"We're perfectly safe, Carol. Just pull up, okay? We'll turn around and rejoin the road well away from that nice lady triceratops, okay? It's not far to the highway now. Just pull up, that's right..."

We roll through a gap between some craggy boulders as we come completely to a halt.

"Uh...*Ryl?*" Harry sounds nervous.

I jerk my gaze to the scene ahead. *"Outage!"*

We're speared by twelve sets of hostile, indignant, slit-pupilled eyes. Recovering myself hastily, I speak lightly, "Uh, I don't think we're welcome here, Carol. Let's just back out gently and turn around, okay?"

"Wh-what..."

"Come on, Carol, let's just leave."

The Dakotaraptors are closing in on the truck, except for the matriarch and her mate, who remain firmly positioned between us and the three nests, giving us the worst evil eye of all. If we don't get out of here right now, the pack's going to launch itself on us with utter disregard for their own safety, and even with two guns, we'll be seriously outnumbered. When it comes to defending nests, raptors are the worst—or best, depending how you look at it. I glimpse Harry readying his rifle out of the corner of my eye.

"Carol, reverse, *now*, or they'll attack us!" I grab the gearstick and ram it into reverse. "Go!"

The pack spring, talons and wingclaws and teeth hooking into our grilles, pulling on them full force. Carol screams and rams her foot to the floor. We fly backwards about a hundred feet and smack into an outcrop of rock. The seatbelt bites painfully into my shoulder as the impact throws me forward and Kiko topples from my shoulder into my lap, screeching in alarm.

Most of the raptors have fallen off, but they're already rushing towards us again.

"Carol, go!" I shove the gear lever into position. "Turn right, back to the road. Then we can outrun them easy-peasy. *Carol?*"

The first raptor is nearing the truck. "Shall I shoot?" demands Harry uncertainly.

"What? Heck, no, we just need to drive off! Carol, go… *GO!*"

The raptor leaps for Carol's window, and we lurch forward as she finally hits the gas again. "*Right*, Carol, go *right!* No, *RIGHT!*"

But she swerves away from the raptors, around the outcrop that shields their nesting ground, heading further from the road by the moment. "Carol, make a big circle and head back the way we came!" A raptor surges alongside Carol's window, cocking its head to peer in at her. "*Carol! Listen to me!*"

I shoot a look at her face: ghostly pale, her eyes bulging and glazed with terror. It's no use. She's not even hearing me.

We lurch and bump over the rough ground, engine revving as wheels lift off the ground here and there. How much more of this can the truck take? Fortunately the ground ahead looks reasonably flat for quite some distance. Maybe once the raptors stop chasing us, she'll calm down.

If they stop. We're barely doing forty over this bad terrain and the raptors are keeping pace easily, ruff feathers puffed out with a mixture of excitement and lingering protectiveness. It gripes me to kill them after we blundered into their nesting ground so rudely, but…

"Let's take a few shots at them, Harry. We're far enough from the nests now it should discourage them."

I press the button to drop the windows and try to line up my rifle on the nearest raptor, but with us lurching and bumping along it's hard just to get my tip safely through the grille. If Carol would stop for a moment, we could scare them off easily enough, now, but as it is…

"Carol, stop, okay? Or swing around and head for the road! *Please!*"

Sweat coats my forehead and trickles down my back. If we break an axle, a drive shaft, a vital bearing… I grab Carol's shoulders and shake her, making us weave slightly. "Carol! Stop! You're going to kill us all!" She just hunches over the wheel even more, panting deeply, her foot rammed down on that gas pedal.

"Carol!" I slap her, but she still doesn't react. The ground is getting flatter and flatter and we're gathering speed.

Swinging back to the window, I shove my rifle right through the bars, with no attempt at aiming, and pull the trigger. At the shot, the raptors drop back, but only to form a tight group immediately behind the truck, out of our line of fire—so they think. They're dropping behind as we accelerate, but this smooth ground won't last, and they'll be on us as soon as we slow.

I grab the emergency hammer and shove it into Harry's hand. "Break the rear window, quickly!"

I hear the click as Harry unfastens his seat belt so he

can scramble into the trunk. Snapping on my safety catch, I drop my rifle tip to the floor and lean over to Carol again, grappling with her, trying to steer us at least slightly to the right. We've got to get back to the road where we can outrun them safely and easily!

A crunching sound, followed by a tinkling of glass, and suddenly I can hear the excited raptor chatter much more clearly. Carol's breathing in sobs, hunching lower and lower. I'm about to reach for my rifle again, unfasten my belt and climb into the back when I see what's ahead.

"NO, CAROL!" I grab for the wheel, trying to steer us away from the crag-encircled bog we're heading straight towards. Carol fights me with deranged strength and from this angle I just can't hold on—the wheel jerks from my hands, spinning hard left and the rear of the truck lifts…then we're rolling, gravity flips, my rifle butt smacks me in the jaw, Kiko screeches, Harry yells in pain…and with a squelching sound, we come to a halt, right side up, for a wonder.

Much good that will do us. Dry rocky ground is visible just feet from my door, but we're in the bog. All four wheels.

Immediately, I glance around, checking our grilles. My chest freezes up.

We are so dead.

HARRY

Breathing raggedly, I push myself up—ow! My hands are cut from all the loose safety-glass crystals I've just been tumbled with, and a spot on my forehead throbs fiercely. Through the rear window, I see the raptors racing towards us, still some way behind, ruffs flaring at the scent of blood.

"Get your gun!" Darryl's voice is sharp, catching slightly.

I look out my window and see…bog? I lurch to the other side…argh, no! We're completely stuck. Then I register how clearly I just saw out of that window. My eyes dart around the truck. One rear grille is completely gone, torn off as we rolled. The windscreen grill is badly crumpled at the driver's side, exposing several feet of crazed windscreen. Carol's grille—not gone, but hanging from one corner so it might as well be. Darryl's is dinged but largely intact, though a raptor could certainly work its head through the gap if given long enough.

In the back, the other one is scrunched sideways but probably still effective and the rear grille looks un-damaged. Much difference that will make. My throat clenches up, tight, and my hand shakes as I grope in the footwell for my rifle.

Even if we can shoot all these raptors before one of them gets in somewhere, what about the next pack?

Eventually we'll run out of ammo. We need to send a distress signal to Highway Control just as soon as a satellite comes close enough. But it will have to wait until we've driven these raptors off. If we can.

Darryl takes a quick look around outside before cracking the door open enough to hurl Kiko up into the air, then slamming it tight shut again.

Yeah, he's got wings. Four of them. I guess he's the only one with a chance of getting out of this.

DARRYL

Carol's still shaking and moaning, but I can't do anything for her now. I ready my rifle, snatching a glance at the WhatHap box. No satellite signal. Darn it.

Hang on...a movement up in the crescent-shaped crags around the bog catches my eye. *Outage.* Velociraptors. Smelt the blood from Harry's hands, no doubt. They're staying back from the incoming—much larger—Dakotaraptors, but poised to dart in and join the feasting if the opportunity presents. One of those won't have to stop and wriggle to get through my window, which means we've got four vulnerable openings to worry about, not three. And two of the last three grilles are utterly compromised.

Anger and helplessness curdle inside me. I knew it wasn't safe traveling with Carol but...what else could I do? Guess I should've insisted she drop Harry at Mau's. Maybe that was the responsible thing to do. Or refused to go unless she let me drive? Too late now.

Too late.

Time to start dropping those raptors; see if we can put them off. Ignoring the cold voice telling me that there are simply too many of them, I'm just getting the lead Dakotaraptor—now only six hundred feet away—in my sights when a most unraptor-like roar fills the air and something huge and grey surges alongside, blocking my view. For a split second my confused eyes take it for some sort of large herbi'saur—then I register the metallic finish and the shape. A HabVi!

The vehicle's side door hisses open and a voice shouts from the cab, *"In, quick!"*

I unsnap my seatbelt. "Harry, go!"

The door clicks and the truck rocks as Harry leaps out, but I'm too busy unfastening Carol's seatbelt. "Carol, come on!" She hasn't even moved!

Why is no one shooting from the 'Vi? I haven't heard anything, no sign we have cover!

"Hurry up!" yells the voice. "Raptors incoming, whaddah-ya-waiting-for!"

"Carol, *hurry!*" I pull on her arm as hard as I can. "Carol, look, it's safe in there, come on!"

She just clings to the steering wheel, rocking to and fro.

"Move, *NOW!*" comes the hunter's voice, vibrating with urgency. I'm taking too long…

"Carol, just *follow me*!" I fling the door open and leap from the truck—surely she'll follow?

I lurch two squelchy paces through the bog and scramble onto the rock. The 'Vi is so close I could touch it. Just a couple of feet to the side door where Harry stands, shouting to me, though I can barely make out his words. But, before I can reach him, raptor calls sound, so close, and the door hisses closed despite Harry's panicked lunge. I've been too slow, it's too late…

A snarling-hiss… I spin around—a Dakotaraptor's hurtling towards me, full-tilt.

My racing mind makes the calculation—I can't raise my rifle and aim in time. Even as my muscles bunch to try, the raptor springs, sailing through the air, killing claws extended, wing arms spread…it'll slit my belly open before it's even carried me to the ground—

Smack!

The cab door of the HabVi swings open, smashing into the raptor and knocking it from the air.

"*IN!*"

I glimpse urgent eyes, a reaching hand, and hurl myself upwards, one foot pushing off the step, my hand seizing the extended one—a yank, and I tumble onto the driver's seat, tangled with my rescuer. Even as I land, I'm trying to sit up. We both turn, grabbing the door handle and heaving as hard as we can—too slow, a ruffled-looking raptor's head appears in the gap, lunging for us. The guy's foot shoots out, slamming into the raptor's nose with such force it jerks back.

We haul frantically on the door and it closes… almost. The raptor's got one wing-claw into the gap. It pulls, terrifyingly strong, and we cling on for dear life. Then, as it eases up for a moment, thinking alike, we both let the door swing open—*just* enough to give us the leverage to slam it *hard*…with a screech, the raptor snatches its wing-claw clear and with one more desperate heave, the door clicks shut.

Only then, panting, shaking, safe, I remember Carol.

"Carol!" I lunge for the door, but the guy touches a control and the lock snicks.

"It's too late!"

I raise my rifle, but my eyes make sense of the scene outside just in time to see the pack racing away into the shelter of the rocky outcrops, dragging…something.

"Carol! O God, Carol!"

They're gone. Not sticking around near a HabVi, even one that isn't shooting at them.

"Why didn't you shoot? Are they asleep up there? Are they—" My voice sounds high, hysterical. I break off, my breathing ragged, my head ringing. Trying to take in what just happened.

"Why didn't she run to the 'Vi?" The guy's face hovers in front of mine, tense, anxious, skin a light, chocolaty brown, like a baby Edmo's tummy feathers, eyes a richer shade.

"Scared. She was scared. O God, I left her!"

"You left it too long as it was. What else could you do?"

I can't answer. There's banging...a hoarse voice... coming from the rear of the vehicle. Screaming my name.

My eyes dart around, finding the interior door control. There's another *snick* as the guy unlocks it—I press the "open" button and the door slides back to reveal Harry, pounding madly on the unresponsive side door.

"Harry, I'm here!"

"*Darryl!*" Wide-eyed, he stumbles three steps and throws his arms around me.

I close my arms around him and cling on tight, feeling the pyx ramming into my chest. That, at least, is safe, like Harry.

"Darryl, thank God!" he whispers after several long, quivering, bone-cracking moments. "*What took you so long?*"

"Carol wouldn't move." The words come out so low it's a wonder he hears me. I glance around the living area. Yes, the shutters are closed for travel, so he didn't see what happened.

"Carol?" He looks towards the cab, but of course, when I can't help glancing over my shoulder too, there's just our rescuer sitting on the driver's seat, watching us. "Where's..." He leans, trying to peep into the rest of the cab, his voice wobbling fearfully... "Where's Carol, Ryl?"

I can't meet his eyes. I look away. "I thought she'd follow me. Herd instinct." Did I? Or did some cold practical part of me just know I had no choice? Move or die. It should've been too late for me as it was, if our rescuer wasn't certifiably insane—or insanely brave. Again I see his foot smashing into that raptor's nose; again a sense of disbelief envelops me as I remember how he *opened his door*. Even after locking Harry in because it was too late. "But...but she *didn't*. Follow me."

Harry swings towards the side door, eyes wide, gripping his rifle.

Numbly, I shake my head. "It's...it's too late, Harry. They...they *took* her."

He wraps his arms around his chest and swallows. "O God. Help her. Someone. Can't we...?"

"Too late, Harry," I whisper.

He draws a shuddering breath, swaying slightly, so I draw him towards me and hold him. I'm too shocked to cry, yet, and I think he is too. The hunter stays silent behind me, giving us psychological space.

Echoey scrabbling sounds from above finally interrupt our silent misery. I look around to see the hunter leaning to check a screen on the dashboard, quickly straightening again, looking more bemused than alarmed.

"There's a distressed quadravian clinging to the tip of the drone dome. Anything to do with you?"

"Kiko!" I release Harry and spring for the ladder to the turret. I'm halfway up before I think to pause and glance at the hunter. "Is it okay if I let him in?"

"Sure. Go ahead. Just raise a window. The piranha'saur mesh isn't down, and he'll fit through the bars."

I'm already spinning the locking wheel on the hatch and pushing it up. I pull myself into the little round room, grab the nearest window handle, force myself to pause and check that there's nothing out there waiting to stick a long, clawed limb through the bars and hurt me, then I push the window up and whistle.

"Kiko? Come on, Kiko. Good boy. Come on in, now..."

His head appears at the top of the window, upside down, anxious eyes peeping at me. Satisfied it's safe, he drops down onto the 'Vi roof and climbs straight up through the bars and into my arms, making soft, distressed, whistling sounds and shaking all over. I seal the window, and it's only when I turn around that I register that I'm alone. The hunter or hunters I assumed were up here don't exist. Is that young guy—he only looks a couple of years older than me—*alone?* What's happened to his partners?

Stomach tightening at the thought of more tragedy, I soothe Kiko until he's prepared to climb onto my shoulder, then I move back to the hatch.

Harry's face peers up at me. "He okay?"

"I think so." I climb down quickly and take Kiko in my arms again, examining him more closely. "Hang on..." Red smears my palm as I run it over the base of his long tail, and he flinches. I part his feathers gently and after some exploration, I locate a long, shallow gash. "He's been grazed. Raptor fang, I guess. He must've landed and had a near-miss."

"There's 'saur first aid stuff in that cupboard." The hunter points to the far side of the living area and Harry hurries across, soon returning with a bottle of liquid-type artificial skin and some antiseptic gel in his own scraped hands.

I'll need to get some human stuff soon and deal with that. For now, I smear Kiko's cut with gel and dab a bit of the artificial skin over it to seal in blood scent.

When it's done, I hug Kiko in silence, trying to quell resentment that he's alive and Carol isn't. It's not his fault. If Carol could've flown away, I'd have chucked her out and she'd be okay too, I guess.

Finally the silence grows too awkward. I look up from Kiko, catching the hunter chewing his lip as though unsure what to say. I make eye contact, but I still can't speak, even to ask for stuff for Harry.

"Was...uh..."—the hunter clears his throat—"was that, uh, your mom?"

"Stepmom," I whisper.

"I'm, uh, real sorry. How come..." His eyes dart over Harry and myself, lingering on the veterinary supplies I've just used, assessing us and concluding "farmers," no doubt. "How come she didn't know what to do?"

"She's...was...from the city. Only lived out here three weeks or so."

"Aw, heck."

"I should've...I should've talked her out of it! I knew she wasn't up to the journey!"

"She could've at least let you drive, Ryl." Harry's voice is small and miserable. "It wasn't your fault."

He's talking sense, but still guilt twists in my belly. Guilt that I left her, guilt that I missed the moment, somewhere back along the line, when I could have prevented this. But I swallow more—useless—self-accusations.

The hunter shifts uncomfortably on the driver's seat where he still sits. "Do you, uh... You got some hair? For a hair burial?"

"Hair burial?" A memory stirs of Father Ben telling me about some hunter custom by that name, but I can't remember the details.

"We keep a pinch of hair from each haircut so's if we...well, you can wrap it in a shirt or some'at and bury it. So's you can have a ceremony."

Yes, that's what Father Ben had said. "We don't have any hair."

"I'm sorry. That's too bad." He peers out the driver's window towards the truck. "I hate to be so practical, but we'd better try and pull your truck out of that bog before dark. If you want it, that is—looks totaled, to me. But it'll have sunk by morning."

"Sunk? Completely?"

"Sure. Look at the angle of the rock sides, there..." He traces the outline with his finger. "It's a pit bog, this. It swallowed a whole 'Vi, twenty years ago, without a burp."

"You're kidding," says Harry.

He shakes his head and touches the Saint Des statue on the dashboard. "Saint Des my witness! Every hunter round here knows 'bout it. They blundered in on a foggy autumn morning when they shouldn't have been driving around at all if they'd any sense."

"Did they...survive?" My throat closes at the thought of raptors encircling the stranded men in their sinking vehicle, 'cause I know *exactly* how they'd have felt, now.

"Well, they scrambled out—no choice, the speed that heavy 'Vi was going down. And they got to dry land and moved fast, up to—can you see, there's a depression in the side of those crags? They piled in there, backs to the wall, guns pointing outwards, and set off a flare now and then once the mist burned away, fending off every raptor in the area as they waited. And they got lucky, 'cause a car on the road saw a flare and Highway Control made it before they ran out of ammo. So, yeah, they survived. Praying to Saint Des like mad the whole time, so they say. Wasn't quite enough to be writ down as a miracle, but near enough."

"I'll say," murmured Harry.

"So, uh, do you wanna try? To get it out?"

"*Try?*" I feel too numb to make a decision, so I stall. "Surely there's no question this vehicle could pull it out?"

The hunter smiles slightly. "Don't underestimate that sucker. When I was a kid, we were parked up on the bluff, other side of the valley, where I was when I saw y...well, we saw this car moseying off the main road and away into the rough country. Turns out it was some idiot city-folk wanting a car-picnic. Anyway, dunno if they thought it was a nice pretty spot or what, but they drove into the bog. Highway Patrol showed up awful quickly and tried to pull them out with their normal patrol vehicle."

The hunter shook his head. "Wasn't happening. Even a little car like that. So a bigger recovery truck showed up. Had a go. Nope. Even with both of them, that car was stuck fast. You wouldn't believe the size of the thing that showed up in the end and got it out. And they had the medium one pulling on the car at an angle at the same time, to break the suction. Heck, it was hilarious. Went on for hours."

"And you didn't help?" I can't help saying.

"Sure we helped. We sat up there the whole time, watching, and the raptors knew we were there and didn't try to jump the temporary fencing Highway Patrol set up—that stuff's never high enough to help for more than an hour or so. More important than going down and leaving them uncovered while we tried to help tow with a vehicle which ain't built specifically for towing."

"Oh, yeah. I guess."

"Yeah. So I'm no-way assuming this 'Vi can pull your truck out. But we can try."

I step forward slightly so I can see through the cab window, staring at the truck. I have to agree with the guy's assessment. It's totaled, all right. Would we even want to fix it? It would be like...I try to cut off the end of the chilling thought, but I can't.

Like driving around in Carol's coffin.

"I don't think we want it. Right, Harry? We can just take a bunch of photos and send them to the insurer. But if we could get our stuff out, that would be good. I packed our birth certificates and things."

"Yeah, my claw necklace is in there," mutters Harry in a flat voice, like that means considerably less to him right now than it usually would.

"Right." The hunter stands up and steps forward into the living area, only to stumble, his jaw clenching. "Ah, darn it!"

"Are you hurt?"

He bends, sliding a couple of fingers inside his boot. He pulls them out—wet with blood.

JOSHUA

"*Outage*," gasps the farmgirl, "did the raptor bite you?"

"Yeah...oh, no," I correct quickly. "Not that raptor. I had a run-in with one a week or two ago, and the wound hasn't been healing right. I guess I split it open again when I kicked that critter just now."

"Are you...alone out here?" She tenses, clearly expecting a grim tale.

My shoulders hunch sheepishly, my cheeks heating. "Uh, yeah. And before you say anything, I know how stupid it is, okay? I've learned my lesson." I gesture down towards my foot with my bloodied hand. "You don't need to say a word."

"So...nothing happened to your partners?" Her face relaxes in relief.

I shake my head. "Nah. My assistant skipped out on me last time I was in the city, left me in the lurch with contracts to fulfill. I couldn't find anyone else, so I came out alone. Bad decision, yeah. I've been moseying around scoping out the prospects for my last contract while letting my foot heal, only it ain't been co-operating. Infected. I was gonna cut it open later and drain it properly, but I think kicking that thing has taken care of that."

"Well, come on." She puts the dinky quadravian up onto her shoulder and steps to me, taking my arm firmly. "Sit down so I can look at it."

Limping badly, I let her lead me to the chair her brother picks up from the floor and sets upright for me. They seem competent, these two.

"Where's the medical cupboard?" She looks around—then seeing the red cross on a cupboard behind her, she moves to it without waiting for an answer.

I watch her inspecting the contents and selecting items with easy confidence. The last thing I really want is to let someone else mess around with my injury, but Dad always emphasized the importance of sizing someone up as soon as possible—regardless of how short a time you'll have them in the 'Vi—and this is a good way to do that. Someone's going to have to go outside in a minute, after all, and someone else provide cover. Anyway, looking after me is calming her right down, taking her mind off the awful loss they've just suffered.

"Okay." She soon sets her choice of supplies on the table I didn't stop to stow earlier when I saw their truck career off the road like that.

For the first time disquiet niggles at me. Did I do the wrong thing, giving chase at once? Should I have stayed up on the bluff and provided cover from there? Nah, one single gun at that extreme range wouldn't have done enough, not against a pack protecting their nesting ground. *Especially* not since I'd been up there for three days and the raptors had been going about their business as usual for the last two of them, correctly concluding I wasn't after them and keeping me well entertained with their family dramas.

"Oh, uh, I'm Joshua, by the way," I say, as the farmgirl pulls two more chairs from the rack and unfolds them. "Joshua Wilson."

"Darryl Franklyn," she says, brushing brown hair from her light-skinned face.

"I'm Harry," says the boy. *Her brother* doesn't need saying, though his eyes are brown to her blue.

"Hi." In the circumstances, I think it best to swallow

pleased to meet you. "Uh, welcome to the Wilson HabVi."

"This is Kiko," Darryl adds, tilting her head towards the expensive pet. I guess she sees what I'm thinking because she adds, "He came to us as...kinda as a rescue."

There's clearly more to the story, since a healthy quadravian's far too valuable to be in danger of being put out on the street, but I accept the real communication with a nod: *no, we're not so stinking rich that we throw money around on such luxury pets.* The story can wait.

She sets out the extra chairs, lifting my foot onto one and sitting in the other to unlace my boot. Kiko remains crouched on her shoulder, his long feathered tail wrapped tightly around her neck, his four wing-limbs sticking out like spikes on a burr. I glance at her brother, hovering, still pale-faced and clammy-looking.

"Say, you see that boiler tap there? Can you get some mugs and things from the cupboard beside it and make us all a hot drink? Well...if your hands aren't bleeding too much."

Darryl shoots me a grateful smile. Glad I'm giving her brother something to do or knowing we all need the drink? Both, probably.

"Sure," mutters the boy, moving towards the cupboard.

His sister snaps on a pair of disposable starch

gloves and nods at the box she took them from. "Put some of those on, Harry."

"Good idea. Ah!" I suck my breath in as she presses—unavoidably—on the wound while she eases my boot free, causing the pain to spike.

"Sorry."

"It's okay." I grit my teeth to hold back any further sound as she peels my sock off, revealing the ugly mess. Blood and pus coat my foot, which is swollen around the deep puncture wound about a third of the way up from my toes. What little of the wound can be seen under the fresh blood is as unhealthy a color as it was this morning, no surprise.

"Oh, uh, washing machine..." I point and she swings the little door open and tosses the gory sock in, followed by the boot.

She wipes blood away from my foot with a sterile wipe, and I barely control a flinch. The blasted thing was hurting enough even before its latest exercise. But when she offers me the box of painkillers, I shake my head. Dang things make me woozy, especially when I'm already on antibiotics.

She looks closer and purses her lips. "Nasty," is all she says.

"Yeah," I sigh.

Her kid brother hasn't got the gloves on yet, too busy watching. "Yucky," he agrees.

Another good distraction pops into my mind. "Yeah, if you look on that shelf there, you'll find the fang that did it."

Harry picks it up at once. "This is yucky too!"

"Yeah, it was an old critter with rotten teeth. Probably why my wound got infected. All the serum I shot in there should've dealt with a normal bite."

"Are you sure there isn't some boot fiber or dirt stuck in there?" demands Darryl.

"I didn't think so when it happened, but that's partly why I figured to slice it open tonight and take a good look, wash it out well. Though it's not easy for me to get a clear look in it. Awkward angle."

"I guess not. Well, I can do that now." She no-nonsensely snaps on a fresh pair of gloves to replace the ones that have been touching my dirty boots and socks, adjusts the supplies beside her, then rips open a sterilized scalpel pack and takes out the blade. "Sit still, Kiko," she murmurs, clearly as a preventative, for the little 'saur still clings silently.

"Hey, kid, gimme a teaspoon from that drawer, would'ya?" I point, and the boy pulls one out and hands it to me. Still ungloved. Making a mental note to wipe the drawer handle with an odor-control wipe later, just to be sure, I place the rubber handle between my teeth. Something tells me this is gonna hurt.

Darryl shoots me an approving look, then opens the

wound properly with two quick flicks of the scalpel. It's sharp, so that isn't too bad, but when she places her hands on either side and presses firmly, it's all I can do not to yank my foot from her grip and kick her across the 'Vi. As it is, I sink my teeth deep into the rubber handle, clutch the chair arms and just about manage not to make a noise as a disgusting quantity of pus erupts from the wound with enough force that Kiko starts back, hunching into his long wing-limbs still more.

"Wow!" Harry stares avidly, revulsion on his face.

"*Ow*, more like." The girl shoots a look at me. "You okay?"

I nod, not prepared to ease up on the spoon when she's clearly not finished. *Argh*. Nope. She squeezes again, harder. More pus.

"This is a real mess," she states. "You should've done this sooner."

"Ugh-uh," I mumble around my spoon, shaking my head, sweat popping out on my forehead. "Dun wanna too quick. Ged more bugs inh."

"Hmm." She squeezes some more. When the pus—finally!—stops coming, she props the mouth of the wound open with the sterile clamp and shines the medical light into it, squirting distilled water in to clean it. She peers and squirts for some time, manipulating the clamp occasionally—*owwww*—to get a good view all around.

"Well"—she finally sets the empty water syringe on the table—"I didn't see anything come out, but there's nothing in there now." She packs the raw hole with antibacterial cream, injects antisepsis serum into the surrounding flesh, puts in a couple of staples to hold the slightly enlarged wound closed, then wipes the surrounding skin clean before sealing the whole thing up with a big chunk of solid artificial skin. One final go with a fresh wipe, then she adds a clean white cloth bandage around it all, just for extra support, and I'm officially blood-free.

"There." She sits back at last, stripping off the second pair of gloves, outside tucked carefully inside. "That's all I can do for that."

I take the teaspoon from my mouth with a shaky hand, feeling sweaty and disheveled, like a dishcloth that's been wrung out hard. "Right. Thanks. You'd better deal with his hands now. We must stink of blood."

An alarmed flicker crosses her face as she registers how much more serious that is outside the safety of her farm fence. "Harry, let me see your hands." She pulls him towards her by the wrists, so I heave my sore foot off the spare chair and wave him to it.

He grabs the teaspoon as he settles—grins and waves it at me. "Yo, you've got one strong bite! Is your nickname Rexie?"

A deep set of toothmarks now scar the rubber, and it's good to see him smile. I grin, too. "Better than bellowing like a laying longneck and distracting your sister from her excellent work."

Darryl gives a dismissive flap of her hand, cheeks reddening slightly. "It's just basic first aid," she mutters, pulling on a third pair of gloves and beginning to clean her brother's injuries. "Don't be a baby!" she adds, holding on tightly when he flinches and tries to pull away. "It's only a few cuts!"

Harry shoots a sidelong glance at my punctured foot, then squares his jaw and sits resolutely still. I press down a smile as I ease off my other boot and sock and toss them into the washer.

After wiping the drying blood from my hand with an odor-wipe, I inspect the floor for any blood or pus, but there's nothing but mud. Can I face getting up to make the hot drinks? Pain still pulses through my mauled foot in nauseating waves, but everyone could do with one.

The farmgirl catches my glance towards the boiler tap. "Don't you dare! You'll make it bleed again!" The words are commanding but her look is one of appeal, so although I doubt I will, what with staples *and* artificial skin *and* bandage, I relax back into my chair and look innocent. She rolls her eyes and bends over her "basic first aid."

There're so many little cuts and grazes—not only on his hands but also on his chin and cheeks, brow and scalp—that I'm guessing he got tumbled with some broken safety glass when they rolled. Guess Darryl still had her belt on. But eventually everything's been cleaned and creamed and, where possible, coated in a smear of liquid artificial skin.

Darryl takes off the latest pair of gloves. "Where do these go?"

"All medical waste into the incinerator. That hatch beside the boiler tap, with the flame symbol. Scalpel and clamps too, they'll get filtered out before they reach the ash tray and sent for repacking."

In it all goes and, as Darryl puts the unused supplies away, Harry remembers the drinks and swings into action. He must've been inside a 'Vi before, because he locates the pull-out worktop beside the boiler tap without difficulty, lines up three mugs and makes tea.

"Hey, Darryl..." She's moving to help with the drinks, not that there's anything left to do.

"Yeah?"

"You got any cuts? Let me see..."

"Oh." She blinks. "I don't think I have."

But she sits in the chair so I can check her over. She does look okay, but I'm still catching the tang of fresh blood in the air. Someone's still bleeding, and I reckon it's her.

Wait...a slight smoothness, a sheen...I slide my fingers into the damp hair behind her ear and she flinches. "Found it."

"Oh." Her fingers rise, touching the sticky area. "I-I hadn't noticed. How'd you know?"

"I could smell it." Couldn't she? She gives me a startled look, so I guess not.

She goes over to the kitchen area and bends over the sink basin under the window, reaching for the faucet. "Nuh-uh," I say, realizing what she's planning. "Use the wipes. Then they can go into the incinerator."

Going red in the face at her gaff, she lets Harry fetch the medical wipes and clean her hair and the cut underneath.

"Yeah, it would be much easier to make a thorough job of it at the sink," I add, trying to make her feel better. "But then we'd have blood in Grey Two, y'see? Uh, you know, one of the wastewater tanks."

"Yeah, I wasn't thinking," she mutters as Harry attempts to get liquid skin onto the cut to scent-seal it, gluing a section of hair to her head in the process.

Heck, now who isn't thinking? How long have we been? Not that we've any choice. Can't go outside bleeding. All three of us are still liabilities as it is—all four, including the quadravian!—and most especially cut-up Harry. I glance into the cab, then slide my chair over to the main console and raise the shutters from the living area's small, horizontal windows. Dusk hangs heavy in the air and the truck has already settled noticeably, the bog pressing over the bottom of the doors. "Where are your bags?"

"Trunk."

"Good." The rear door, although hinged sideways, is higher than the side doors and still accessible. "Let's do this. We can have the tea after. You two get up in the turret with your rifles and close the hatch. I'll squelch over there and get your things."

"What?" Darryl's eyes widen in protest. "But your foot... I should go!"

"How heavy are your bags?" I slide my chair to the washer and press "start" to deal with the last of the blood then begin pulling my gum boots on—carefully. "Can you stand over there and throw them clear into the 'Vi?"

She bites her lip, shooting a glance out the window, measuring the distance. "It would be pushing it."

Her honesty raises my estimation of her competence another notch.

"Then I'd better go. It'll make it a quicker job in the long-run and that means safer. If you two are good shots, that is?" I wouldn't usually accept cover from strangers, but they've impressed me so far. And there's probably gore in the truck, if nothing worse. Kinder not to let them get too close a look.

"Darryl's a crack shot!" Harry pipes up proudly.

"Harry's not at all bad, for his age," Darryl adds.

"Okay, then. The crags are too close, yeah, but the raptors won't be in a hurry to rush a 'Vi. But they need to know this 'Vi means business, 'cause they've got too used to me being around the last few days. So, no 'oh, it's only looking.' Now's not the time for that. Shoot the first thing that moves and shoot to kill, and I doubt we'll have any further trouble. I mean, the first identifiable raptor," I amend, just in case they misunderstand.

A fleeting do-you-take-me-for-an-idiot look crosses her face, but she must realize I'm just being responsible by saying that because she simply nods.

Harry huffs, though. "What, like we're going to shoot some baby edmo just 'cause it peers at us? Or are you saying we're *not* to shoot an allosaur if one turns up?"

Darryl rolls her eyes. "Up the turret, Harry. Come on, quick. It's getting dark."

She pauses as she moves towards the ladder herself. "Say, is there anything in this critter cage? Kiko doesn't like gunshots."

"Nah, it's empty. Pop him in."

The little 'saur makes unhappy noises as she detaches him and shuts him safely away, but it's me — or rather my foot — she's shooting worried looks back at, as she follows her brother upstairs.

I wait until they've shut the hatch before getting to my feet. *Ow.* But it will carry my weight, and I don't want to take painkillers that might make me fuzzy-headed, so I'll just grit my teeth.

I reach up and press the button on the scentBlocker wall spray, releasing a very large dose to try and camouflage any lingering blood smell from inside the vehicle, standing directly under it so it mists me too. Then I check the main console, swiping through the view from all the cameras and heat sensors, but I can't spot anything out there. I could drag myself up the turret and release the drone, send it out behind the crags to check for heat signatures, but since I'm sure there'll be some raptors hanging around, it's a waste of fading daylight. We just need to be quick.

With a few taps, I set the sensors then touch the com pad to speak to the turret. "I've set the movement sensors to cover the open area, so you can concentrate on those crags. Unless you hear a *dong*, obviously."

"Got ya." Darryl sounds calm; unfazed at the task ahead, which reassures me, and Harry returns a perky "*Yo.*"

My rifle will only weigh me down and get in my way, and I'll only be outside for moments, so I won't waste time putting on scentBlock cream—s'not like it really works on raptors. After a few gentle stretches of my foot to loosen it up, I move to the side door, refusing to limp—much—and touch the com pad there. "Are you ready up top? Hatch locked? All the windows open? Muzzles through the bars? Looking mean?" Hopefully the stronger blood scent wafting out from them, safe up there, will distract from me.

"Yep, we're good. Nothing's showing itself at the moment."

"Good. Remember, first thing to so much as peep—shoot it."

"We will."

"Right, I'm going out then."

I tap the door "open" button then sit in the doorway and drop gently to the ground, good foot first. Less than two strides take me to the edge of the reeking bog and wading two more steps gets me close enough to grab the trunk door. One rear corner of the truck is deeply scrunched—probably from reversing into that outcrop outside the pack's nesting ground—but the door swings open okay.

Three carryalls and a few miscellaneous tote bags.

Perching on the bumper to avoid getting stuck in the mire—*ouch*—I grab the first carryall and toss it accurately through the side door. Then the second, then the third. I glimpse a cage and another tote bag in the rear seat, so I scramble in, crystals of safety glass grating under the reinforced knees of my pants, and move them to the trunk.

As an afterthought, I move further in to grab the statue of Saint Des from the dashboard, pulling it free of its sticky pad. The driver's seat is as messy as I feared, and bloody toe prints around the broken, grille-less window show the entry point clearly enough. I've no time—or need—to look more closely, so I check the glovebox for paperwork, retrieving a driver's license and ID card which I shove in my pockets for safe keeping along with the statue.

Climbing back out, I lob the cage through the 'Vi door, then gather up the rest before squelching back to land.

Crack.

A rifle speaks—Darryl's, from the caliber. A screech and something topples from the crags. I resist the urge to stop and look, simply shoving the bags in and hauling myself up after them. Only when the side door is closed and locked do I peer out through the windshield. A dog-sized velociraptor lies motionless on the slope, a light breeze ruffling its feathers.

"Good shooting," I call, hearing the hatch opening.

"Hard to miss at that range," is the modest reply.

I shrug as she reaches the bottom of the ladder and opens the critter cage to retrieve the lonesome quadravian. "Well, I think I got all your stuff, anyway."

Her eyes run over the bags, lingering on the tote

bag I pulled from the back seat, her face tensing. Guess it's her stepmom's. They've had such a rotten day. I should feed them and get them to bed. Yeah. I can feel my own antibiotic- and infection-weighted body already trying to shut down for the night.

I ease off the muddy boots and put them beside the side door, causing Darryl's eyes to make a dismayed circuit of the living room and turret ladder, everywhere she and Harry have tracked bog. The whole 'Vi stinks, but at least it's a natural scent and not city-smell.

I wave a dismissive hand. "Forget that. We can clean tomorrow. I'll fix something for us to eat." I move towards the kitchen area, barefoot, though I'm limping worse now the adrenalin is wearing off.

"I can do that," says Darryl, popping Kiko back onto her shoulder, where he hooks a wing claw firmly into her hair and licks her ear with his little tongue. "You sit down. Just tell me what you want."

I intend to insist, but somehow I find myself back in my chair, watching as she throws together a simple meal with her brother's help cum hindrance.

"I can do something..."

"Just sit down and rest that foot! Getting a meal is the least we can do, after—" Her face goes grim again.

I'm not used to people cooking for me. With Uncle Z, if I wanted anything but a heart-attack steak I had to cook it myself, and none of the three assistants I've had since I lost him have done anything other than sit and stare at me like hungry calves, waiting to be fed. That's the last thing I want to do to my guests, but even Harry laughs and waves me back when I try to get up.

Darryl soon coaxes Kiko into my lap to avoid feathers dropping in the food, and I stroke the cute critter as I sit and try to relax.

Being alone has been too like that grim time right after Uncle Z... Still, it's weird having company after so many days on my own.

Weird, but nice.

HARRY

By the time Darryl and I have the meal almost ready, Joshua's chin rests on his chest and he's snoring softly. I guess he must be on antibiotics. They always make me sleepy as heck. Kiko remains curled in his lap, calm at last and sleeping too.

Hopefully Darryl will wake the hunter, though. He seems really nice, but I'm kinda in awe of him. Of how tough he is. How he insisted on getting up and *going outside* only minutes after Darryl had finished cleaning out his wound. How he's stayed in the wilds, alone, even after being injured. Hunters have to be tough, I guess, but...well, I thought we'd been raised to be hardy, but I wouldn't have waved those painkillers away before having someone do what Darryl did to his foot.

Moving around the table, I trip over my carryall for about the third time, so I pick it up and place it on top of Darryl's and Carol's.

Carol. I've been trying not to think about her, because every time I do it feels like my insides are in a food processor. What would Dad say if he knew we'd let this happen to her? Okay, it was her fault, but...but...I *tried* to scare her back at the house. I even mentioned triceratops. What if it's really *my* fault she overreacted like that?

Oh, why didn't she just get out and run to the 'Vi?

I can't stop thinking about it, now I've started. Did they kill her in the truck or was she alive when they carried her away? And Dad? Was he still alive when that raptor started dragging him through the fence?

My stomach turns over at the thought. Am I actually going to get sick? I grab the back of Joshua's chair for balance, and he starts awake.

"Huh?"

"Oh, uh, sorry. Um, where's the...the head?" That's what hunters call the toilet, right?

He points to the left of the cooking area. "That door there."

I open a funny corrugated door to reveal something the size of a small cupboard. How do I...? Hang on... My recent tour of West, Thiago, and Ed's 'Vi comes to my rescue. I pull on the door and it extends, until with a little flick I can throw it into a semi-circle, where it locks in position, enclosing some of the living area for extra bathroom space. I spot the toilet seat on the wall and fold it up into position, the tough flexi-plastic "bowl" hanging beneath it. As the hinge moves, a cover on the floor slides back, revealing a hole underneath.

I lean against the wall and run my hands through my hair. My forehead's gone all cold and clammy again. But I really don't want to up-chuck. Not when Darryl and Joshua will hear me. Especially Joshua. It's too humiliating. I look around the little room, trying to distract myself.

There's the showerhead. A smaller covered hole on the floor will be the plughole. The used shower water will go to a special greywater tank and get re-used by the washing machine or dishwasher. Only final rinse water is fresh, and even that comes out of a separate tank than the drinking water, though it was probably pumped from the same stream. Drinking water gets filtered and sterilized. Everything's designed for efficiency in these vehicles. And avoiding smells.

I peer down the toilet hole, but there's nothing to see, though I know whatever drops in goes straight to the incinerator. The nausea's eased and I can't stay in here any longer, so I use the toilet in order to justify my visit, clean my hands—or the artificial skin that coats most of them—and go back out.

DARRYL

I eat hungrily, though guilt lards every bite, making it taste like dust. Carol would think we didn't care if she saw us chewing away like this. I do, but after all the work and stress and everything, my body's very insistent.

Harry eats ravenously too, though Joshua munches with less enthusiasm. But it's probably the infection in his foot dragging him down, not my cooking. I hope! I'm no doctor, but I reckon he's chancing it, staying out here with a wound like that. But then, he's alone, which is beyond chancing it to start with.

He's either slightly mad, or so used to living like this that he thinks nothing of risks even farmers would shrink from. Or a bit of both.

I eye him surreptitiously, still trying to figure him out. In some ways his life experience obviously out-weighs mine by far more than our age gap—and he's tough as rex-hide, no doubt. But there's a freshness and innocence in his eyes that I've never seen in a city-boy and rarely see in a farm kid even Harry's age.

I glance at the photo frame on the wall, now displaying a picture of two young men who look like brothers—and look quite like Joshua, too, though slightly darker skinned—one of whom carries a baby on his front in an old-fashioned carrier. Was Joshua raised out here in a 'Vi? That might explain a lot about him. It's very unusual, though.

Hunters are probably split about thirty-seventy between those who got bored with city life and turned to hunting and those born to it. But "born to it" only means their fathers took them on hunting trips now and then once they were "old enough," whenever their family decided that was. Virtually all hunters keep their families either in a hunter "camp," as they term their often rough and ready fenced settlements, or in the city—or at least on a farm—so their kids always grow up SPARKed—but I've yet to see a single photo to suggest that Joshua did.

I sit and watch the photos cycling past as we wait for Joshua to finish, the two men and the child growing gradually older, clothes and equipment more up-to-date, because it's better than letting my own thoughts fill my mind. Eventually Joshua slowly chews his last bite, swallows and looks up, blinking sleepily.

"Hey, sorry, y'all waiting for me? These antibiotics make me slow in the evening. Let's have one more hot drink and then I'll find you some bunks."

I jump up to forestall any attempt at tea-making on his part, making him grin resignedly. When I set the mugs on the table, he just smiles and murmurs, "Thanks." But after a few sips, he sets the mug down and glances at the main console.

"Say, I should've let you use the console already. Send a mail to let your dad know you two are okay, at least, and I'll bring you home in the morning." He rummages in his pocket with one hand, looking down as he tries to get something out. "Well, unless you'd rather, uh, tell him face-to-face tomorrow. If he won't worry that he doesn't hear from y'all tonight. A message is a hard way to hear, uh, *that*. Or I can set the alarm to peep if we get a lock-on, and you could try to call him." Whatever he's struggling with comes free. "Here, I got his license and ID from the truck. I guess he'll be wanting them."

He plops the two items down on the table. Dad's face looks up at me and tears blur my eyes, my throat strangling me as I fight to keep my composure. Harry sits rigid beside me.

Joshua reaches for his tea—then freezes as though he's just sensed a raptor stalking him. He looks up, his brow creasing. "What did I say?"

I swallow hard. Harry's head hunches down, like a turtle retreating into its shell.

"Uh..." My voice catches and squeaks, so I clear my throat. "Uh, Dad doesn't need them. He...uh...a raptor snatched him this morning." I say the words quickly.

"He's dead. That's why Carol decided to take us to Exception City like that."

Joshua's eyes open wide with horror. Then his gaze flicks to the photo frame, filling with sadness. "Heck," he says at last. "I am so sorry. This must be, like, your worst possible day *ever*."

His commiseration is awkward, but it's overwhelmingly sincere.

"Yeah, it's...it's been a bit that way. Though I guess it would've been even worse if you hadn't showed up."

He shrugs this away. "So, uh, where *do* you want me to take you tomorrow?"

"Home, I guess. To our farm." Earlier, I was so desperate to stay, but now I'd give anything to be in Exception City—with Carol. Still, we can go home. A silver lining that's hard to appreciate right now. "We don't need to use the console. I doubt anyone's even missed us yet."

Wait, should I have told him that? We've only just met him. But there's nothing but sympathy in his eyes as he looks back at me. He's a real straight-up guy, I'm sure of it. Kiko's certainly snoozing happily on his lap, despite the pocket-rummaging, clearly sensing no bad vibes. Anyway, if he tried anything, we could just stamp on his foot, right?

I nod at the two cards in front of me. "Thanks for saving these, anyway."

He fishes something from the other pocket, setting our Saint Des car statue in front of me, where it promptly topples over, unbalanced by the remains of the sticky pad on its base. "I grabbed this too."

I pick it up and close my hands around it for a moment with a silent prayer of thanks to God and the saint for Harry's and my safety—and for Carol and Dad. Then I pass it to Harry, who's been unusually quiet throughout the meal. He clutches it tightly before slipping it possessively into his pocket. I don't begrudge him it. I've something far more precious inside my jacket.

I picture our arrival at the farm tomorrow, alone. So much work to do. Mau and Riley and everyone will help, of course. We'll need to find someone quickly, though. I'm not eighteen for another year and a half, after all. I eye Joshua. He's running his own 'Vi, right?

"Joshua? I guess you're eighteen, then?"

"Huh? Yeah, been an adult for about six months, 'cording to those city-folk."

"Yeah, well, I reckon *we'd* better have a legal adult around or someone official might cause problems. Would you consider staying and doing some easy jobs while your foot heals up?"

Joshua looks startled.

So does Harry—then he brightens. "Yeah, that's a good idea!"

Joshua runs a hand through his hair then scratches the tip of his nose. "Uh...well, I've never really thought about farm work. But, uh..." He shoots a glance down at the table—or maybe through it, towards his foot. "Hmm."

"It would only need to be a month or so, until we find someone. Maybe not even that long. I'm sure Uncle Mau—he's our neighbor—will know a suitable person. You can stay in the staff apartment or in your 'Vi, as you like."

"Well..." He squints so doubtfully at me that I'm sure, foot or no foot, that it's pity for us, not any real liking for the idea, that makes him say, "Well, why not. But you'll have to tell me what to do, and I'm not up for running around just yet."

"There're plenty of jobs that won't trouble your foot. And Mau and Riley—our other neighbor—both reckon the fence is safe enough. It was a million-to-one freak accident."

Joshua looks unconcerned by this reference to our possibly compromised fence, despite it being our biggest barrier to hiring people in future—but then, he's used to having none at all. Harry's face falls again, though, and my heart falls with it. No Carol and no Dad. Joshua's right. This is the worst day ever.

"How did the raptor get in?" Joshua asks, a spark of professional curiosity pushing aside the sleepiness in his eyes.

I shrug. "It's a mystery. Well, not really. We found the gory holes in the fence. But how a Dakotaraptor could've fitted, let alone got Dad through—it ties my head in a knot. But Mau's right—we've seen enough critters squeeze through tiny gaps that we simply have to believe the evidence. But it still seems impossible."

Joshua cocks his head. "Oh, they can squeeze through the darndest gaps when they want to. But how come it didn't trigger the alarms?"

"Pure bad luck. It broke three wires, but the fence is only alarmed every five strands, and the first and fifth didn't get broken."

Joshua's look grows more intent. "And it didn't trigger any alarms by jiggling it?"

I shake my head. "*Nothing*. All the readings were normal. Dad must've thought nothing had got through, 'cause he got out without taking his rifle."

Joshua frowns. "A *three-wire* gap and it didn't shake it enough? A *Dakotaraptor*? I'm astonished it could get through a gap that size. How old is the fence? What's the spacing?"

Hang on... I have an expert tracker sitting in front of me, ready to explain this mystery if anyone can! Raised in a 'Vi? Entirely possible he's the best tracker in the whole state. "D'you want to see the photos?"

"Sure." Joshua sits up, interest clearly well engaged,

and slides his chair to the console. "I'll ping your band, just accept the lock and send them over."

Soon he's swiping the photos of the fence hole up onto the screen, eyeing them, then zooming in here and there. From the way his eyes dart about, focusing on this and that, he's seeing a world of information that's invisible to me.

After a while, he sits back and frowns. "Got any pictures of the, er, the site of the attack?"

"What, didn't I... Oh, I thought I'd sent them." I ping the other half of the photos to him, and he starts his staring and zooming and frowning again.

Finally, he just sits, leaning back in his chair with his hands knitted behind his head. Still frowning.

Eventually, Harry can't take it any longer. "So, how'd the critter get in?"

He stares at the screen for one more long moment before turning to face us, his expression deadly serious. "Okay, look, what I'm about to say...it may not *change anything*, you need to understand that..."

"Change anything?" demands Harry. "What do you mean, *change anything?*"

"I mean, your father *could* well be dead. And..." —he waves to the screen—"a Dakotaraptor was certainly meant to take the blame. But...well, he wasn't killed *there*. Only taken."

"Taken?" I repeat, stupidly. *Taken?* But taken

means...

"Yes, taken. And *yes,* that does mean he *might* not be dead. But no way to say from looking at this whether it was a kidnapping or a kidnapping swiftly followed by a murder in some more convenient location. Which- ever, it was no carni'saur that did it. It was a person."

Two thoughts ricochet around my mind until it spins.

A *person?*

Dad might be alive?

He might be *alive?* I stare at Joshua. "How certain are you?"

Despite his seriousness, a hint of amusement touches his confident eyes at this question. "Absolutely one hundred percent."

My heart pounds, harder and harder. A steady thud of hope.

Dad may be alive!

O God, Saint Des, Mother Mary...

Please?

Please, please, pleeeeeease?

====+====

DON'T MISS

unSPARKed 4

FARMGIRLS
DIE IN CAGES

After the tragedy that has shattered their lives, Darryl and Harry are keen to return to their farm, allow their new friend, hunter Joshua, to hunt for clues about their Dad's fate, and to start rebuilding their lives.

But soon unexpected threats force them to drastic action. And their decisions may have far-reaching consequences for them all.

OUT NOW!

Read a SNEAK PEEK!

Find out more at: www.UnSeenBooks.com

DARRYL

Birdsong wakes me. Loud birdsong. Anyone would think they were sitting in the attic this morning, singing at the tops of their voices just on the other side of my ceiling! I open my eyes but despite the birds it's still pitch black, not a trace of light filtering through the shutters. Weird.

I snuggle down, meaning to go to sleep again, but as I pull the quilt up to my chin something cold and jangly brushes my wrist. I twist my hand and grab it. A zipper?

Why am I in a sleeping bag?

Memory strikes—like stepping under a waterfall. An icy waterfall.

I'm not at home. I'm in a Habitat Vehicle. Joshua Wilson's HabVi. The eighteen-year-old hunter who saved my brother and I yesterday evening.

But not Carol. Or Dad, snatched yesterday morning. Both dead.

No. *Dad...*

Dad may in fact *not* be dead.

I sit up in the utter blackness—*ouch!* Muscles twinge across my chest and back and shoulder. I guess that's from the seatbelt. Carol rammed us backwards into an outcrop pretty hard, even before the truck rolled clean into the bog. I feel around the walls for a light switch and my hand touches a control panel by the door, near my feet. I stroke it in a clockwise motion and a glow comes from the ceiling, getting brighter as I move my finger.

I'm in what hunters would grandiosely term the Habitat Vehicle's 'master bedroom'—a small compartment seven feet long, about three or four foot wide and the same high. Various cupboards and drawers line the walls, and a rack on one wall holds my rifle, on top of which my quadravian Kiko is roosting, his four wing-limbs still tucked up around him as he peers at me and blinks in the sudden false dawn.

Small, but I'm certainly not complaining. It's undoubtedly the best the HabVi has to offer, and I was embarrassed when Joshua insisted on moving his sleeping bag and a few clothes to the cab 'bedroom' and tossing a spare sleeping bag in here so I could have this 'room.' But I didn't argue too hard. Hunters have a whole culture of their own and although Joshua's shown no inclination to doubt my competence simply due to my gender, I've a hunch he's required to give me the safest berth in the vehicle, no discussion.

Joshua had already moved the 'Vi about two hundred feet from the bog, his jaw tightening as he operated the pedals with his injured foot. "Don't want a longneck or some'at large to knock us in there in the night, do we?" he said, parking in the shelter of a large rocky outcrop.

He then cleared some things from a top shelf-bunk over the kitchen area to make a space for Harry and found him another spare sleeping bag before giving us a quick run-down on how to use the shower. Disappearing briefly into the "bathroom" himself, he soon reappeared, damp-haired and clean-clothed, and yawned his way into the cab, clearly exhausted by the metabolic load of the antibiotics and infection battling it out inside him.

I didn't think I'd sleep for hours, after Joshua's revelation about Dad—kidnapped! Not dead, kidnapped!—but Harry and I only went over it about three times while I cleaned my rifle before we both started nodding at the table.

Obedient to Joshua's firm instructions—"we can't do anything about any traces of blood smell from all these cuts but we can wash off all that tasty mammal sweat"—we take it in turns to pop into the tiny bathroom and shower, slipping on our own nightwear from the bags Joshua retrieved earlier from our bogged-down, smashed-up truck. Joshua's bloodied socks and boots had finished washing, so I took them out and bundled all the dirty clothes in and started it off again, the way he'd asked me to.

And then we finally got to bed. But tired or not, I lay awake for a good hour, staring into the absolute darkness of the secure, windowless berth, listening to Kiko's soft breathing and thinking about Dad.

Dad's all I can think about this morning, too.

Kidnapped! Not dead, kidnapped!

Okay, I correct myself firmly. *Maybe not dead.* Joshua was very clear about that after inspecting the photos of the scene.

"No way to say from looking at this whether it was a kidnapping or a kidnapping swiftly followed by a murder in some more convenient location."

Yeah, sobering observation. Still, there's a chance!

I look around the compartment again, then slip into clean clothes from my bag, which I slung up here last night. I pick up my outer jacket very carefully and put it on, feeling the shape of the pyx pressing against me from the inner pocket. It made me uncomfortable leaving it there overnight, but what else could I do with it? Despite the Saint Des statue in the cab and the pictures in the living area and the turret—in fact, the saint's looking down at me from beside the door in *here*, too—there won't be a tabernacle on board, and Joshua had already gone to bed so I couldn't ask him for advice.

I've not noticed any crucifixes, crosses, fish symbols or other statues, anyway, so there's no guarantee he knows much about anything other than Saint Des. Reverence of Saint Desmond the Hermit is well on the way to becoming a folk religion in its own right, among hunters. Father Ben once told me it was a delicate balance between encouraging them to make more direct contact with the Almighty *as well* and simply being grateful they were reaching out to Him *at all*.

"They *get* Saint Des," he explained. "All the complicated theological stuff, well, it goes over their heads. But living in a cave surrounded by danger, trusting completely in God for your safety? They really *get* that."

Easy enough to see why, I guess. Plenty of hunters have his statue and ask his prayers, say his chaplet, without even being Catholic. There's even an official hagi...hagi-something—saint story—that Saint Desmond's diocese commissioned a decade or two back to try and quash all the tall tales that were circulating. I read it the other year and the truth is extraordinary enough. I bet Joshua has a copy on his hand-pad.

Unless it was the two guys from the photo frame—his dad and uncle, I'm guessing, though he's not mentioned them yet—who had—have?—such a strong devotion. But the fact that he took the time to retrieve our car statue suggests he has at least the usual hunter's appreciation for the Patron Saint of All Those Who Live Out-City.

A slight noise penetrates the somewhat soundproofed 'bedroom' from the living area. Is it

Joshua? I wanted to ask him a thousand questions last night about Dad, but he said we should discuss it properly in the morning. Guess he was asleep on his feet.

I pat my shoulder—Kiko springs across onto it, so I take my rifle from the rack and shuffle along to the door. I try more of a swiping movement on the control panel and the screen glows into life, showing a view of the living area. Oh. It's Harry, not Joshua. From the way he's hopping around clutching his foot, he disdained the foot holds and leapt all the way down from his bunk, a far enough drop for an adult hunter and he's only a thirteen-year-old farm boy.

I spot the "open" button, press it, and the door slides back. "It's a metal floor, Harry. That wasn't smart. Are you hurt?"

Harry stops hopping at once and adopts a *pain, what pain?* expression that can't fool his big sister. "I'm fine. Just jarred it. It's nothing."

"I hope it's not." Joshua's agreed to come back to the farm with us and help out until we can employ a more experienced man, but the last thing we need is him *and* Harry lame.

Not wanting to repeat his mistake—though, thanks to the higher head height in my berth, the drop is less— I slide out backwards and find the foot holds to ease my stiff self gingerly down, then pull out my rifle and let the door slide closed. Propping my gun next to Harry's, I look around the small room, all robust, easy-clean metal-fronted cupboards and folding furniture. HabVi's are never as large inside as you'd expect, because so much of their walls consist of storage space.

The cab door is closed.

"Is Joshua up?"

"Not that I know. S'pect he's crashed out." He stares at me for a moment, and I half expect his next words to be 'What's for breakfast?' But he says, "D'you think Dad's alive?"

I bite my lip. Shrug. "I hope so, but I guess Joshua's right. There's no way to know." We've already gone through this three times last night, but it's like a scab. You can't stop picking at it.

"Who would take him? Who would want him dead, come to that?"

"I don't know, Harry." The question makes me feel tired, though I've just got up. "I couldn't think of anyone last night and I can't now. It makes no sense."

No sense at all. Yet...we've got to figure it out. Dad's life may depend on it.

JOSHUA

I still feel heavy and slow when I open my eyes, but my head is clearer. When I sit up on the seat-bed—Uncle

Z's bed I can't help thinking of it, 'cause this was always his room—and feel my foot, it's a lot cooler than it was last night. Hurts less when I flex it, too. The latest treatment has hit the infection hard. Hopefully it will heal up, now.

From the light filtering through the shutters, I've slept past dawn by about an hour. My guests—employers-to-be, 'cause I didn't dream that I agreed to go live on a farm for a few weeks, right?—will be wanting breakfast. And information. Everything I can tell them about their father's kidnapping. I refused to get into it yesterday evening. We were all far too tired and stressed.

I sit up, stretch, then look at Saint Des's statue, on the dashboard. *Did I do the right thing, Saint Des? Saying I'd work for them?*

I don't get crazy-stressed inside a farm fence, the way I do in a city, but it sure wasn't something on my to-do list. All I wanted was to get my triceratops calf, go back to the city once my foot was better and find a new assistant. Not that I ever exactly *want* to go in-city.

Never mind. It's only for a short time and those kids have just lost their step-mom as well as their dad. No telling if or when they'll get him back, even if he is alive. They're good people, and I'm happy to help them out, even if it's mostly just with my over-eighteenly presence. City-folk have funny ideas about the age of eighteen and adulthood and all that.

I pull on clean clothes, tucking the others inside the sleeping bag to wear a second night before washing, take my rifle from the rack on the inner wall and go through into the living area. Darryl and Harry both sit at the table, holding mugs, and from the empty bowls they've been pro-active enough to solve the breakfast issue by themselves.

"I made oatmeal," says Darryl. "I hope that's okay."

"Only if you made me some, too," I say, with a grin to make it clear I'm teasing.

She grins back and nods to the stovetop.

Sure enough, there's a portion of oatmeal in the bottom of the pan. I almost open my mouth to let her know that the food processor would've produced perfect oatmeal and kept it at the optimum temperature, too—but she might think I was criticizing her efforts so I just smile and ladle it into a bowl. It's slightly warm, still, so I make a cup of coffee and sit at the table without bothering to reheat it.

They've worked out how to raise the living area's shutters, too, and a glance out the window confirms that their truck has sunk into the bog in the night. Only the closest side of the roof still peeps above the muck and even that is much further from the shore than it was last night as the vehicle slides inexorably into the deeper part.

I catch the look Harry shoots Darryl—and the little headshake she sends back—but the atmosphere is tense with expectation as I eat. Sure enough, I've just swallowed the last bite when Harry bursts out, "So, are you sure Dad's alive?"

Get FARMGIRLS DIE IN CAGES from your favorite retailer today!

DON'T MISS

Elfling

SHE MUST FIND HER FATHER… OR DIE.

Alone on the streets of London, young Serapia Ravena seeks her father, her only hope of survival. But he hides a dark secret, one that threatens his very life and his very soul. The search for his salvation will carry Serapia to the very heart of the wild places and bring her face to face with her own mysterious heritage. If you love tales of redemption and second chances, good and evil, elfin and dragonets, you'll love this heart-warming fantasy in the tradition of J.R.R. Tolkien and C.S. Lewis. Winner of the 2019 'Teen' Catholic Press Book Award, ELFLING also spent a month at No. 1 on Authonomy's 'Editor's Desk.'

Buy the book to enter Serapia's world today.

"I was instantly drawn in"
EOIN COLFER,
author of ARTEMIS FOWL

Out Now!

Read a SNEAK PEEK!

Find out more at:
www.UnSeenBooks.c

CHAPTER 1

Raven

I was hungry. So hungry that most twelve-year-old girls of my rank would have been crying, throwing a tantrum, or fainting. Perhaps all three. Not me. I was thinking what to do about my hunger. I began each day with the same all-consuming thought.

I sat on a thin blanket under the overhang of an old, crooked stone house near Smart's Quay. I had to bend my head to sit up, but I scarcely registered the minor discomfort. Rain splashed from the eaves to the cobbles of the street only a few feet in front of my nose, but under here it was fairly dry; a good sleeping place. I contemplated the various possible solutions to this particular morning's hunger, until a tiny scuffling noise preceded a whiskered nose from a narrow crack in the wall. When I remained motionless, the rat scurried almost soundlessly to the side of the blanket, attracted by a few crumbs so tiny even I hadn't noticed them.

My hands shot out and seized the rat, wrapping around its plump body. Ignoring the squealing and the snapping teeth, I gripped the head and twisted, feeling the sudden give as the vertebrae in its neck parted company. Laying the twitching rodent beside me, a rare smile snuck onto my face.

So early in the morning and I had already acquired my day's meal! I would take the rat along to the Water Lane cookhouse, where I would skin it, cook it, and eat it. The bones would go to Old Joe the gluemaker as payment; the skin to the skin man in return for a precious half copper. In the new language I had learned since my mother's death, a half copper equaled a piece of bread. If I was extravagant, I would eat it for supper. Otherwise it would go some way towards staving off the hunger on the morrow.

The smile fading, I shuffled to one side, picked up the blanket and knotted it around my shoulders like a cloak. The rat I tucked out of sight in my jerkin. I wriggled out into the street, straightened and froze.

Two urchins stood waiting. Unlike me, who merely dressed as a boy, these were actual boys, bigger than I. Born in the gutter and never slept on a feather bed in their lives. They would cut my throat for the rat.

"We heard a squeaking," said one boy, holding out a hand, his eyes cold.

"Do you see anything?" I said—running even before I had finished speaking.

The boys followed close on my heels. So close that when my bare foot slipped from under me on a slimy cobblestone the first was on me immediately. As I fell I caught sight of a mangy dog lurking by the side of the street. I struck the ground painfully, one hand already inside my jerkin. The boy landed on top of me, a knife appearing in his hand like magic. Dragging the rat free I flung it towards the dog, which moved in a brown streak. The urchin had a choice of cutting my throat or getting the rat. It was no choice at all; he was already in mid-air after the meal. Back on my feet even as the rat struck the ground, I bolted.

I stopped in the comparative shelter of a lopsided building off Lowe Lane, wet, tired and sore. I didn't bother contemplating the downturn in the day's fortunes, too busy checking over my clothing. My knees and elbow were badly bruised, but nothing was torn, so I headed for a disreputable inn I knew where the landlord did not keep a porter on and usually allowed me to earn a few pence carrying the luggage.

When I arrived outside the Fylpot Arms, the cheap coach was throwing out a passenger at the door. It was nothing personal; that was just how the cheap coaches went about things. The passenger, having gained the cobbles, ducked as his two cases were thrown down beside him. The coachman flogged his broken-down horses for a good few seconds before they were convinced to move and the coach swayed unsteadily away through the wet streets of London town.

I was already in motion. Stopping beside the passenger I put on my stolid, dependable expression and, with a tug of my forelock, took hold of the cases.

"I'll get those, sir," I said, in my feigned gutter accent. Was it really feigned? When had I last spoken as myself?

The traveler did not want to spend money on a bag boy, I could tell. He had planned to carry them quickly into the inn himself. Recoiling from appearing miserly when actually put to it, with a poor attempt at grace he gave me a curt nod and entered the inn, looking back only three times to check the luggage was following.

I dragged the heavy cases up the stairs, appreciating why the man had ducked their descent from the coach top. But my scrawny frame was up to it, and I set them down carefully in the room and waited. I only ever stuck my hand out as a last resort, it frequently seemed to do more harm than good. The traveler noticed my continued presence with a flash of irritation, dug a coin from his purse and threw it in my general direction.

I caught it and left quickly. It was a good-sized copper, and I was hungry enough that I went straight down to the inn kitchen and swapped it for a half copper and a chunk of bread. Retreating to the inn courtyard to eat my meal and watch for the next traveler, I eyed another urchin lingering there. Did he also have the landlord's permission to carry bags?

The bread was finished all too quickly, as always, and I sat wishing another traveler would arrive. More at that moment for the distraction from my own thoughts, than for the coin I could earn. Only when I had some amount of food in my belly was I troubled by thoughts of the future. It was the only time I could afford to be.

I had lasted three years on the streets, three long, painful years since my mother died and my uncle threw me from the place that had always been my home.

"Be gone, witch child," he'd snarled at me, "or I'll duck you in the pond till you're clean and cold."

Even at nine years old I'd recognized a death threat when I heard one and I hadn't tried to go back. Of course, I had always known my uncle hated me, but to be thrown from my own home to what should've been almost certain death? It had been utterly unexpected. The house in which my uncle now lived was mine, was it not? My rank came to me from my mother and there was nothing legal to take the property away from me.

Legally, though, my uncle was my guardian. No doubt he assumed me dead long since and it was a fair assumption. *Serapion* the urchin had no more chance of reclaiming what belonged to Lady Serapia Ravena than the morning's rat had of breathing again.

In fact, Serapion the urchin had only one chance in the world and it was tied around my waist, carefully concealed under my clothing...

I looked up as the kitchen staff burst from the doorway, chattering excitedly to one another and followed by the cook, who swept something ahead of her with an expression of grim courage. They were calling for the landlord and I darted over to see what the to-do was about, slipping to the front. I'd have seized any distraction.

The heap of ash was tipped over the doorstep onto the cobbles of the yard. The landlord came striding out of the building even as I crouched to peer more closely at the tiny creature floundering weakly in the midst of the soot. As grey as ash, it resembled a bird, for it had a curved, beaky upper lip and a pair of little things that were clearly undeveloped wings on its back. But it was entirely featherless and had two tiny front paws, just now making feeble movements in the ash. Fragments of broken, blackened eggshell lay around it, showing it to be newborn. Or rather, new-hatched. I had never seen anything so intriguing.

"A demon-creature, sir, a demon-creature in the fire..."

"I was sweeping out the grate, sir, and I sees it..."

"It ain't nat'ral, sir, ain't right..."

"Shall we have a priest, sir? Don't like the thought of it otherwise..."

A priest? Whatever for? I'd sensed evil often enough, and there was nothing of it here. But I'd learned long ago that other people just didn't seem able to sense things as I could. Even my mother couldn't. I had stopped mentioning my strange sensitivity only a short time after learning how to talk about it at all.

The landlord leant over to scrutinize the 'demon-creature'. "Evilest looking blighter I ever did see," he pronounced, "but soon sorted." He raised his foot. His intent was obvious.

The baby animal raised its head and peered around with a pair of huge golden eyes. It gave a little cough and a cloud of ash came from its beak. It must be half choked. Without even considering it, I reached out and snatched it from the path of the landlord's foot.

The assembled group turned a look of astonishment on me and the landlord swelled with rage. "You impudent little..." He took a step towards me.

For the second time that day, I ran for my life. Or in this case, the life of the creature I held pressed to my chest. I would survive a beating, it would not.

The landlord did not pursue me beyond his inn gates, but his furious shout followed, ringing in my ears. "If you *ever* come back..."

An inn without a porter was rare. One where I was trusted to carry bags was rarer still. I had lost the closest thing to a real job I had ever achieved, and for what? A deformed chick? I must be mad. Panting and heart pounding, I slipped into an alley off Lyme Street and sank down on the cobbles to take a closer look at just what I had saved.

My hands were filthy with soot and the chick, or whatever it was, still grey, so that must be its natural color. It could not be a chick, I realized, as I looked more closely. Apart from its four legs it also had a tail, a very lizard-like tail. Its little, clawed front feet scrabbled gently at my thumb in a way that reminded me of a mouse. It could hold things in them, I suspected.

It was, I concluded with a sense of shock, some rare exotic creature from across the seas. How its egg had come to end up in the inn fireplace was a question I did not even bother pondering. But if it was rare and from far away, then it was worth an enormous amount of money.

I looked at the tiny thing again. It fitted snugly in my palm, leathery hide soft against my skin. I'd never get close enough to the nobility to sell it for a pet. I'd have to sell to a middleman and it would go to an apothecary to be dried and powdered for potions. And much as I usually ignored the fact, I was terribly, achingly lonely. The creature raised its head again and gave another little cough, and I knew I could not sell it. It was mine and I would keep it. It would not eat much.

Talking of food... I looked again at my new companion in distress. It would need milk, or something. I tucked it securely inside my jerkin for warmth and set off once more along the streets, giving Fylpot Lane a wide berth. Reaching Puddinge Lane I climbed up some abandoned scaffolding to the rooftops and entered the attic of a deserted house through a hole in the roof. The rotten floor groaned under my weight, but I moved lightly to a pile of old rugs in a dry area of the room. There, curled in a little nest, lay a cat and her five kittens. The mother cat regarded me warily with yellow eyes, but did not run or move to attack. The cat and I had shared the loft on many a night.

Now I put my handful down carefully at the edge of the nest and crouched there, watching, ready to snatch it back out if the cat tried to harm it. This was a very longshot, and I knew it. The creature was unlikely to know how to get to the food on its own, for one thing, and the mother cat might try to savage it if it got close. I'd probably have to catch the cat and hold her down while carefully guiding the lizard-chick to the teat. But I wouldn't do it immediately when there was just the feeblest chance I wouldn't have to shatter the trust that existed between us.

The lizard-chick peered around, coughing again. Its babyish gaze travelled from me to the mother cat and it swayed forward unsteadily, opening its beaky mouth again to let out a soft, quavering cry not unlike those of the kittens. The mother cat went on watching me, seeming scarcely aware of the intruder now easing its way slowly, but persistently, in among her brood. Finally the lizard-chick's mouth closed around a teat and it began to swallow. Every so often it released its mouthful to give the kittenish cry again. The cat still did not react.

I watched in something close to wonderment. The mother cat hadn't noticed the interloper, of that I felt sure, and the back of my neck prickled in the way I associated with my odd senses. My new pet intrigued me more and more.

Although I usually avoided staying in the same sleeping place for more than one night at a time, I remained in the loft for over a week. By then, desperate to sleep elsewhere, I began to consider coming to the loft in the daytime to let my pet feed. But my problem was solved when my casual offering of a crumb of bread was eagerly swallowed by the lizard-chick.

"You don't need milk any more, huh?" I said, stroking under the soft leathery chin. "Well, time for a name, I suppose."

I turned my pet around in my hands. I had already established as well as I could that the lizard-chick was female, something most young noblewomen could not have done. Now I considered the question of a name. The baby was still a uniform grey all over, apart from her beautiful golden eyes.

"You are quite like a bird," I mused softly. "And you're mine. I'm a Ravena, in name, at least. Ravens are black not grey, but you're close, and there are girl ravens as well as boy ravens. I'll call you Raven. Then you're part of me."

CHAPTER 2

Winter's Tail

I huddled into my cloak and blanket, shivering, and pressed closer to the chimney wall at my back. That blessed spring weather had been swept away by a very nasty sting in winter's tail. I needed more food. Food was money, though. Raven fared better than I did in cold weather, of course, tucked away inside my clothes, not only for warmth but also kept from prying eyes.

I touched the ring tied so carefully around my waist. I hadn't been out to the palace this week, but I knew I could not go. Not until this weather broke. I could spare neither the time nor the energy. It wasn't as though I had ever heard so much as a *word* about the Duke of Albany. A man I had never seen, nor knew anything of, but whom I believed to be my father.

Not that it was conclusive in the slightest. In my entire life, no one, not my mother, nor my own maid, nor any of the other servants, had ever mentioned my father to me or even in my hearing. There was an obvious conclusion to be drawn from this, even by a well-brought up girl, and I had eventually reached it. Astonishing as it might seem, considering my pious and impeccably behaved mother, I must be illegitimate.

Which might have explained my uncle's dislike for me, had it not been for the fact that he liked my mother. Though I'd sometimes wondered how genuine that liking really was, when all his visits seemed to end with my mother giving him money. But only after he had paid his deathbed visit had I, for the first and last time, heard of the Duke of Albany. My mother had been almost gone by then but had insisted upon seeing me again, probably, I now suspected darkly, because my uncle had divulged his intentions, leaving her in desperate straits regarding my future.

Only then, in such dire necessity, had my mother spoken of this man. And only a few words. A few words—and a ring—pressed into my shaking hand.

"Go to the Duke of Albany," my mother had whispered, and with her last breath, "he will look after you..."

Of course, going anywhere as an urchin was far from easy, let alone going to find a man one did not know and had not the slightest idea how to find. Initially, I had naively believed I could seek help from one of my mother's few friends, sure they would have a carriage harnessed for my conveyance to this Duke's residence. My already disheveled state and the common belief I was with my uncle on his country estates had denied me access even to the upper servants and brought threats of what would happen if I persisted in my 'lies'. Before long, survival left me with no time to worry about the Duke of Albany.

Thanks to Siridean, and later kind old Father Mahoney, I had slowly mastered my new life and eventually managed to take up my weekly pilgrimage to the one place where I thought I might hear of, or even find, this elusive Duke. The old gossips that hung around the Courte Gate could be guaranteed to know all who had attended court in the past week, and all the scandals of my old world. But it had been over three years, and I had learned nothing...

Another urchin, slightly bigger than me, but thinner, was coming along the backstreet, shoulders hunched and shaking with cold. As he came level, his eyes darted to me. His desperate eyes.

I rose to flee just as he lunged. I raised my arm before my face and swung it sideways, feeling the jar as my wrist struck his, but his other hand reached my throat, or more specifically, the fastening of my precious cloak. I felt it come loose and hurled myself forward, knocking him to the ground.

We struggled in a breathless silence. He landed several blows to my head and took advantage of my disorientation to break free and flee. With my cloak. I sat up, willing my head to stop spinning, and wound my fingers into my blanket. I'd tied it over my shoulder, like an ancient Roman's toga, and it had not come free as easily as the cloak.

Raven chattered a warning and I looked up quickly. A much older boy walked rapidly towards me, staring intently at something that lay in the mud. I struggled to focus on that tiny circle of gold.

My ring!

Raven shot forward, and the boy and I dived after her. My hand closed around the ring and I twisted halfway to my feet, turning to grab Raven and flee. But... *Oh no!*

The boy held Raven. He had his hand wrapped around her long neck, and her body dangled. Her head twisted helplessly against the circle of his fingers, but she could not bite.

"This'll fetch a tidy penny," said the boy. "I'd rather 'ave the trinket, though."

I looked at the ring in my hand, anguished. It was my only hope.

"The 'pothecary won't care if it's alive, 'long as it's fresh," the boy sneered. He took hold of Raven's body and began to pull. Raven's head tilted up and her legs flailed. He would break her neck!

"Stop!" I gasped. "Stop, you can have the ring!"

I held it out carefully, my other hand extended for Raven. With the utmost caution and mutual mistrust, we carried out the swap. I stumbled backwards several paces, out of immediate reach, Raven clutched to me.

"You jus' gotta be a girl," sniggered the boy.

"Am not!" I retorted, with suitably boyish indignation.

The boy shrugged. "Ain't short of coin now," he said, grinning at me and twiddling the ring between finger and thumb. "I can do better than you, anyway. Master Simmons don't bother with the likes of you."

He won't bother with you for long, if you boast like that, I thought to myself. The boy had lifted one foot and turned the heel of his boot to reveal a secret compartment. He placed the ring inside, closed it, smirked at me and left. I sniffed in disgust. If I had a compartment like that I certainly wouldn't show it off, even to a helpless urchin. I'd need boots first, of course. Now that I thought about it, he probably had the compartment to keep things from his Master Simmons. Lunatic. Even I had heard of Master Simmons. And stayed well away from him.

Shivering twice as hard, I made my way to Fenchurch, to a small area of greenery tucked behind a triangle of houses. I sat down with my back to the high, encircling wall and stared despondently at the grass in front of me, with its great stone cross towering in the centre. The pauper's graveyard was too recent to have been built over. On Sundays there might be poor folk there, placing some single flower on the communal grave. Some urchins would take these and sell them to the next person, and so on, until they wilted.

Today it was quiet and I could sit there alone, shaking with the shock of my loss. *What do I do now?* A comforting warmth stirred in my nape in response to this desolate question, although no answer presented itself. Raven pressed her face to my neck, making soft cheeps of apology. I stroked her gently. It wasn't Raven's fault.

Sometimes I came to this particular graveyard to escape the bustle. After Siridean had died they'd tossed him in there, with everyone else who couldn't pay for better.

I drew my dagger and held it in my hands, my thumb rubbing around the pommel, cleaning away the protective layer of mud. Hematite gleamed underneath. The shiny silver stone passed well enough for plain steel when strategically daubed with muck. I stared down into it. For a long time, until I found Raven, the dagger had been my only friend. The eyes were there today, looking up at me out of the stone. They looked like Siridean's eyes. I hugged it close, remembering the last time I'd felt as bereft as I did now.

Selling the dagger had been the rational thing to do. I couldn't eat the stone, and a plain dagger would surely do just as well. So I'd reasoned. I'd felt miserable about it, though. Misery turned to pure panic the first time I tried to hunt something. I'd never missed so badly before!

I fled to the quiet cemetery and threw the new dagger at a sapling over and over again. I hardly hit it once. What was the matter with me? I'd chosen a dagger that felt almost identical in my hand: the shape, the length, the balance.

It didn't make the back of my neck prickle, though, the way Siridean's dagger did when I held it and concentrated on my target. The harder I'd concentrated, the better my success. Siridean had taught me the importance of concentration. But I concentrated until I thought my head would explode, and still the new dagger would not fly true. It was then I accepted that the eyes I'd often seen looking back at me probably weren't just a trick of the light. Siridean's dagger had been a very special gift. It had kept me alive this long, and now I had sold it. I felt near despair.

I went back to the shop with the coins, though the shopkeeper would not have bought if he didn't think he could sell it for more, so I held out little hope of being able to buy it back.

But the man answered the door with dark-shadowed eyes and wild words. "Such a night! Such a night I have never had!" He thrust the dagger at me and snatched the coins. "Take the cursed thing and be gone with you!"

I had appreciated the dagger much more after that. It had forgiven my ignorance and come back to me. I doubted I would get the ring back so easily. Common sense whispered that I would never get the ring back at all, but I couldn't accept that. To accept that would be to accept that I was an urchin and would never be anything else, other than an inhabitant of the latest pauper's graveyard.

If *only* he'd put the ring into a *pocket,* I might have been able to get it back. It was just barely possible, anyway: but only just. He'd surely know better than to let me get too close. But a *boot compartment?* How was I supposed to get into that without him noticing?

A movement opposite drew me from my thoughts. I tensed, peering, my hand shifting its grip on the dagger. A dog was slinking from the undergrowth—a big dog, but thin-sided—and limping, which was probably why. One look at its hunting stance was enough to bring me to my feet in a crouch of my own. It sniffed my scent and showed its teeth in a silent snarl. I eyed it back, just as intently.

If I let that thing get to me I'd be in trouble. I touched the hematite and my resolve strengthened. The dog still advanced, head low and teeth bared. There was definitely nothing wrong with its teeth.

Wait, I cautioned myself as it came closer, wait... Its muscles bunched to rush me, and I threw the dagger with all the force and concentration I could muster.

Staying safely where I crouched until it had stopped its demonic howling and thrashing, I then advanced carefully to reclaim my dagger. It was my stomach's turn to growl, and I looked the animal over with rather more interest. Thin, but large, which meant there was still plenty of meat. It might keep me alive until the weather broke. But even this could not raise my spirits by much. I'd lost my mother's ring. Why would the Duke of Albany listen to me now?

I shifted the dog slightly with the point of my toe, considering how best to proceed. The entire dog would be quite heavy to carry, but I would keep the skin and bones and not lose a ha'penny of its value. It wasn't like I wanted to leave any of it behind; even the offal was valuable sustenance. I would just have to carry it. Reluctantly, I reached for the knot on my blanket, to undo it and use it as a makeshift bag.

Again a movement drew my eye. I looked over to the streets and saw the boy who'd stolen my ring. I stiffened, ready to leave the dog and run, assuming he'd followed me to try and get Raven after all. Then I realized he was turning and walking away. I hesitated, torn. A dead dog would go nowhere towards the price of the ring, but if I could ever hope to get it back, I needed to know where the boy was to be found.

I dragged the dog quickly into the bushes and concealed it as well as I could, hesitating one last time. All that meat! Another stray dog might well find it in my absence, but I left it and hurried after the boy.

He walked purposefully, and the streets through which he passed were familiar to me, making concealment easy. Trying to follow someone without it being obvious to everyone else around was rather less easy, but I'd had cause once or twice before and managed well enough.

Eventually, I peeped around a corner to find that he'd stopped in a little back square behind Seethinge Lane and was speaking to a man. I eyed the man suspiciously. He had rather yellow hair and a youth with feral eyes much like the dog's prowled nearby, watching everything. The square was deserted.

"...Y'know Ralph Fletcher were taken for cutt'in that purse? 'An the throat with it?" the boy was saying.

"I know Ralph Fletcher's got himself in jail to hang just after I paid him to do an extremely important task, aye," the yellow haired man replied malevolently.

"Aye, your honor, well, I know'd what Fletcher were good at," the boy continued, "and if you were needing a one for such jobs I thought you might..." he dropped his voice and spoke rapidly for a few moments.

He wasn't just boasting. That was Master Simmons. Time to go.

I made to ease back out of sight, but even as I did the boy turned and pointed directly at me. So much for my unobserved stalking.

Master Simmons' head rose. "Wait." He hooked a finger at me.

I bit my lip but did not dare to disobey. I advanced warily. The boy accepted something from Master Simmons, writhed fawningly and left. The feral youth was still there, out of earshot but close enough. Still...slightly better odds. Numerically, at least.

"Well, boy," said Master Simmons, when I stood before him. "How does this take your fancy?" He held out a fat gold piece.

I stared at it, more enthralled by the sight of gold than I had ever been in my life. That tiny thing would buy back my ring.

"Thomas tells me," Master Simmons went on, when he saw he had my attention, "that you are uncommonly accurate with a dagger over a long range."

My insides began to curdle and I shrugged as non-communicatively as I could. I had a feeling that precious coin might as well have been on the moon.

"Do you know a man," asked Master Simmons, "called Sir Allen Malster?"

I swallowed. Everyone knew Sir Allen Malster. He was one of the Queen's special agents, and he'd seen an awful lot of men like Master Simmons tried and executed. I shrugged again.

"I would be very happy...*this* happy, in fact," Master Simmons twitched the gold coin, "if Sir Allen were to suffer a very accurate sort of accident from a very discreet sort of range."

I swallowed again. "I jus' killed a dog, s'true, sir," I replied. "But the dog were terrible fierce, I'd never even ha' tried, else. I'm glad I hit it 'cus I'm terrible hungry, but it were a surprise, sir." I shrugged as though the implication of my words were obvious.

Master Simmons' hand closed around the gold piece. He might suspect the true reason for my modesty, but he would not risk a bumbled attempt.

"What a shame," he said, with one of the most insincere smiles I'd ever seen. "You'd best go eat your dog." He turned away in brusque dismissal.

I was only too happy to get back to my dog and away from him. I hurried off, resolutely trying to turn my mind to the matter of the dog's preparation and consumption. But before I'd gone very far, my niggling conscience spawned an idea that was not easily ignored. An idea about how to acquire at least part of the ring's value. An idea that made my mouth dry with fear.

My conscience told me that I ought to warn Sir Allen Malster. And my head told me that he might be grateful enough to pay for details. I tried to shake the thoughts away. It was absurd. People were probably trying to kill the man all the time. And money would do me no good if Master Simmons found out.

If I could manage it without being seen... What did I really have to lose? If I couldn't find the Duke soon, I probably wouldn't be alive to do it at all. And finding the Duke would be of doubtful use without the ring. I swallowed very hard.

The dog would have to wait a little longer.

GET ELFLING FROM YOUR FAVORITE RETAILER TODAY!

ABOUT THE AUTHOR

Corinna Turner has been writing since she was fourteen and likes strong protagonists with plenty of integrity. Although she spends as much time as possible writing, she cannot keep up with the flow of ideas, for which she offers thanks—and occasional grumbles!—to the Holy Spirit. She is the author of over twenty-five books, including the Carnegie Medal Nominated I Am Margaret series, and her work has been translated into four languages. She was awarded the St. Katherine Drexel award in 2022.

She is a Lay Dominican with an MA in English from Oxford University and lives in the UK. She is a member of a number of organizations, including the Society of Authors, Catholic Teen Books, Catholic Reads, the Angelic Warfare Confraternity, and the Sodality of the Blessed Sacrament. She used to have a Giant African Land Snail, Peter, with a 6½" long shell, but now makes do with a cactus and a campervan.

Get in touch with Corinna...

Facebook/Google+: Corinna Turner

Twitter: @CorinnaTAuthor

Don't forget to sign up for

NEWS

&

FREE SHORT STORIES

at:

www.UnSeenBooks.com

All Free/Exclusive content subject to availability.